WASTING TIME AND RESOURCES IN MISSISSIPPI

A Novel by Gary H. Baker

D1414377

For Squirrel, Possum, and Songbird

Jeremiah 33:3

"Call to Me, and I will answer you and show you great and mighty things, which you do not know."

Part One

CHAPTER 1

Sometimes a man needs to get up off his duff and do the one thing he was meant to do. I had put it off for years and years and then finally, one day, I decided to open the gate. I decided to let it flow. I decided to change my existence. When a man decides to change his existence, it could go several different ways. He could be very quiet about it, not make a big show. It would be mostly internal changes. I guess you might call them spiritual changes. Or, you could have changes that were cataclysmic; might bounce the needle on the Richter scale. And I suppose, there could be many variations that would float somewhere between those two extremes.

In my case, I didn't feel like I was in great need of spiritual change. I was very comfortable in my old-fashioned Christian faith. I felt like my leaning on God and my acceptance of Jesus as my Savior many years ago were the foundations of my existence. So, it looked like my efforts to introduce genuine "existence change" into my life were going to be more along the lines of convulsive misadventure. Maybe not cataclysmic. But who knew? I didn't.

I remember the day all of this started. It was early in the morning. I donned my running shoes and ran four miles. I had a favorite trail that started in the woods and dropped down near the Cumberland River; close enough to pick up its breath of fish, snakes, turtles, waterfowl, and occasionally diesel fumes from lumbering river tugs pushing up to 1,500 tons of cargo on the big river barges.

A lot of folks said a sixty-eight-year-old man shouldn't have been out in the woods alone, running alone, in the first place. I never paid much attention to many of my friends and family who continually advised me to reduce my vigorous running routine to something less damaging on my deteriorating bones and joints. What did they know? They weren't runners. Anyway, it wasn't my bones and joints that blew up that day. It was my heart.

I had run the first mile and a half nice and slow, probably around fifteen minutes. It was a crisp fall day, mid 60's, the leaves turning golden, burnt orange, dull brown, and a lustrous blood red. I remember the exact shades because, well … because I thought, just for a minute, they would be the last colors my eyes would ever see on this Earth.

The pathway through the woods opened up to an old cattle trail alongside the river. I picked up the pace all the way to the halfway point where I would turn around and start on the two miles back to the house. Everything was fine. I remember hearing three or four dulled shotgun blast from a dried up, late season corn field probably at least a quarter mile away. It was nothing unusual – dove hunters in middle Tennessee in the fall.

In another twenty strides, things were not fine. At first, I thought it was vertigo. If you've never experienced a serious vertigo episode, I don't even want to tell you how scary those things can be. But on this day the problem started as nausea and soon I had a menacing tightness in my chest which I quickly rejected as nothing to worry about. Over the years I had run through a surprisingly large assortment of pains, discomforts, and injuries. Runners get used to these things. So, I plodded on back towards the house. I almost made it. That's about the time I went down and laying there on my back I began to regard the intensity in the coloration of the leaves. I experienced a new level of amazement and awe. Have you ever thought about what would be going through your mind when you believed you might be dying? All I could think about were the trees around me – the great and mysterious forest. Each tree was a life force which somehow had a message for me. The messages were all jumbled together, but the one which spoke the loudest said, "You better get up off the ground right now. If you don't, you never will." Others said, "You are weak, your blood is like iced tea, your muscles like torn spaghetti."

I listened to the loudest tree. I got my ass up off the ground and ran as hard as I could the last eighth of a mile to the house.

I live alone. My wife, Sarah, passed away six years prior. She was as good a person as you'd ever find on this sad and stunning planet. The first two or three years without her were tough. Many days I didn't know what I was doing. Many days I didn't know much of anything. I had always thought that if she went first, I'd go back to drinking, but I didn't.

So, I was back at the house and trying to decide whether or not I ought to drive myself in to the E-room. I was pretty sure I'd just had a heart attack. I thought about old Dorcel Taylor. He was a second cousin to my father. Dorcel had spent many an oppressive sunbaked day behind the haunches of a mule. Scratching out a meager living as a sharecropper wasn't easy. He was as good as gold, and just as "country" as anybody from the deepest, darkest hollers of Alabama, Georgia, Mississippi, or Kentucky. Thinking about Dorcel, I remembered what he told me one day. We were at a hog-killing. Dorcel was pretty old, at least eighty, so his attendance at the festivities was honorary, strictly social. Six or seven much younger and stronger men would be performing the time-honored rituals themselves – the killing, the scalding, the scraping, the gutting, and the butchering. Those activities would eventually produce the succulent rewards: tongue, brains, lard, cracklings, tenderloin, hams, ribs, bacon, sausage, ears, and feet.

My presence at the annual tradition was based purely on earnest curiosity. Although my distant cousins performing the ritual were bred to it, I grew up in the city and was never a part of this established practice of rural America, this hog-killing.

Dorcel and I were enjoying the show. It was early December and the show was performed on the banks of a swift-moving spring-fed branch. We were chatting about some old timers who had recently passed on, raising the question of whether Dorcel and I actually had some other obscure blood connection, besides the one with my father. In the rural south, these kinds of conversations occur quite often. We were sitting in a couple of old scraggly lawn chairs and Dorcel was leaning forward just a bit, his big bare hands resting on his knees. I noticed a scar on his right hand just about halfway between the bend of his wrist

6

and his worn and withered knuckles. Actually, there were two scars there, both about a half inch in length and separated by an inch.

"Dorcel, where'd you get those scars?"

"Snakebite."

"You're kidding."

"No sir."

"What happened?"

"I was pickin' blackberries one mornin'. I reached down real low to grab a couple … bam! A rattler hit me hard."

"I guess you headed off to town to find a doctor, huh?"

"Well, no. I didn't go to town a'tall."

"You didn't go see a doctor?"

"No, I did see the doctor, but he wasn't in town."

"Somebody went and brought the doctor back to you."

"No sir. The doctor was right there all along."

"What do you mean?"

"Well, you see, the Almighty Doctor, the Great Physician, He's all we ever need to be healed. That's what I done. I went to Him and He healed me."

"You didn't get sick or anything?"

"I reckon I was a mite weakly for a couple of days. It shore did swell up pretty good. But He took care of me. God was all I needed."

"Dorcel, that's amazing."

I didn't tell him *how* amazing it was, and how privileged I felt that he'd shared this story with me. But I've never forgotten it and I was thinking why do I need to see a medical doctor today? Why not be like Dorcel? Why not trust God to heal me? After all, everything is done on His timetable, not ours. If I'm supposed to drop to the floor from cardiac arrest in the next sixty seconds, that's God's decision, not mine. Also, if I was supposed to live another twenty years, that was God's call as well, not mine. I got to thinking, another twenty years? I'm sixty-eight now, I'd be eighty-eight then. What could I possibly do in those years that would be productive, useful, worthwhile? What could I do that would remove me from the normal, predictable onslaught of old age – the lethargy, the lost hope, the boredom, not to mention the ghastly and visceral decline of my aging body?

That's when it came to me – what I would do to change my existence.

The first thing after my coffee the next morning I went for another four-mile run. There was no nausea this time, also no chest pain. Thank You Lord. Thank you Dorcel. When I got home, I fried a pound of bacon and whipped up a three-egg cheese omelet. I carried the food and coffee back to my desk and sat down to think about this new existence I was about to create.

I knew what it was going to be, this new existence. I knew what it might look like. I knew the one primary activity I would be involved in. I knew the inspiration to begin this activity was solid, was real. I knew I was going to do it. I knew I was going to jump in and let it all hang out. What I didn't know was exactly how to get started. I was going to have to think it through, apply some discipline to the planning. I sat there at my desk in deep thought, deep meditation. After a while, I realized my eggs and bacon were cold. I hadn't touched them. I gave the eggs to Shirley, my cat, and I gave the bacon to Oscar, my black lab. But I still had not figured out the first steps I needed to take in order to jump-start my new existence.

Write it out, my inner voice said to me. *Write it out; take a look at it, make any corrections that are necessary, then submit it to the newspaper and post it online after you figure out the correct website or even better, build your own website.* Here is what I wrote out in longhand and then typed it in my computer: Christian Counselling   615-476-0946

Two words and my cell phone number. There it was, the pathway to my "New Existence". I phoned the two largest newspapers in my area, *The Tennessean* in Nashville, and *The Leaf Chronicle* in Clarksville and asked for classified advertising. The ad for a monthly was $65 at *The Tennessean* and $49.85 at *The Leaf Chronicle.* I paid, over the phone, with my debit card and was told the ad would begin tomorrow. I was in business. But really, this was not going to be a business, this new existence of mine. There would be no profit motive. I couldn't bring myself to charging a fee for a service I'm sure Jesus himself never charged a fee for. And He was the best Christian counselor the world has ever seen, right? Of course, I'm right.

The practical side of me said people would understand if I charged a modest fee. After all, I was bound to incur expenses along the way. And what about the value of my time? People would understand. Surely they would. But deep down inside, I knew better. This new existence of mine wasn't about paying the rent. My new existence was going to be different. Also, I felt like I'd been blessed abundantly in my sixty-eight years on Earth. Now it was time to give back. What would Jesus do? He'd give back. He'd already given everything, but still, He'd give more. He'd give back. And that's what I was going to do.

That evening I called my son, Aaron, who lived two hundred miles away, near Knoxville. "Hey", I said.

"Hey, what's up?"

"Nothing much, just wanted to say hi. Everybody okay?"

"Yeah, we're fine. How about you?"

"Hanging in there. I've run four miles each of the last two days."

"Don't overdo it. You haven't forgot the vertigo, have you?"

"I'll never forget it."

We were both quiet for a moment. "Really, I called to give you a bit of news."

"Uh, okay."

"I'm starting up a little venture. No money involved, just a service, I guess. I've been thinking about it for a while. There's something you might be able to help me with."

"Tell me more."

"I'm going to provide free Christin counseling to anyone that answers the ad I put in the paper. But I don't know if I'll need a website or not. What do you think?"

"Christian counseling... uh ... yeah, I could see you doing that. As far as a website, I don't know."

"I don't either. Guess I'll just wait and see what kind of response I get from the ads. I put one in The Leaf Chronicle and one in The Tennessean."

"Dad, have you thought about liability?"

"What do you mean?"

"You know, human nature being what it is, some upset, angry client might bring a professional malpractice suit against you."

"I don't think I'd worry about that. I'm not a professional."

"Exactly."

"Okay, I see what you mean. I'll look into that."

"I would if I were you."

We talked a little more about his three kids – my grandchildren – and his wife, Crystal, and that was it.

"Good night, Dad. Love you."

"Love you too, son."

The next morning, I didn't go running. I needed a break, plus, I was fired up in anticipation to see if I'd get any responses from the classified ads I had placed. I wasn't so fired up that I didn't go through my morning rituals. I fed Shirley and I let Oscar out of the house. I knew where he'd go to sniff around and how long it would take for him to return. He couldn't get in much trouble where I live. My closest neighbor is a quarter mile away. I let myself out of the house also. I like to walk around the edge of the woods and although I don't have to lift my hind leg to take care of business, I hold dearly the freedom I enjoy to do whatever it is I want to do on my own property. I don't believe it gets any more American than that.

When I came back in the house, I put on some water to boil for oatmeal and poured my first cup of coffee for the day. A few minutes later, I was at my desk when my cell phone went off. It was 8:15 a.m.

"Finn Weaver," I said.

"I'm calling about the Christian counseling."

"Oh, yes. How can I help you?" The caller was a female and if I had to guess, I'd say she was under thirty.

"Well, I don't know how your service works, or anything, but I sure could use some help."

"I see. You called the right place," I said as I grabbed a pen and notepad. "Could you give me your name and tell me a little about what's going on?"

"Don't you want to know if I can pay you? That's the first thing they ask, I mean the other counselors I've called."

11

"That's not going to be an issue with me. I won't be charging you anything. You see, my service is set up on the premise that Jesus didn't charge anything for his counseling. I'm not going to either."

"That's awesome. Okay, my name is Renae Holsclaw."

Before she continued, I thought I should let her know. "Renae, I've never actually been a counselor before. I'm a retired basketball coach. You're my first customer, uh, I mean client."

The line went silent. I thought maybe I'd run off my first potential patron. I waited to see if she was going to hang up. She didn't.

"You said your name is Finn?"

"That's right. Short for Finnegan."

"Finnegan Weaver, right?"

"Yes."

"I remember you. You coached at Austin Peay. I'm not much on basketball, but I remember your name."

"Good. Look, I may not have credentials to call myself a counselor, but I've been honest with people my whole life, and I want to help people. Give me a shot. I'm sure I can help you."

"Coach Weaver, you don't have to convince me. I couldn't find anybody else that would talk to me. I'll be glad to be your first victim."

CHAPTER 2

I only had one other call that day that asked about the counseling. When I told him I had no credentials or experience, the caller said thank you, but this isn't what he was looking for.

I'm not dumb. I knew there would be skeptics. I also knew this is what I was supposed to be doing, and that God would connect me to the people He wanted me to help.

As for Miss Holsclaw, we had talked for half an hour. As it turned out, my guess that she was under thirty proved accurate. She was twenty-five. She had an eleven-month-old daughter, but she didn't have a husband. She had a court date looming, but she didn't have a clue as to how to convince the judge she couldn't be sentenced back to jail for her recent third conviction on marijuana possession. The court date was actually a sentencing hearing on that recent third marijuana conviction. Renae told me that if she had to go back to jail that she would lose her daughter. The state, Human Services, would step in and take control this time. The last two times they had acceded to Renae's request to allow Renae's aunt to take care of the little girl while Renae served her six-month incarceration in the county jail. There was no one else, family or otherwise, who could care for the child.

This new hearing was three weeks away. Renae was getting close to the panic stage. She knew if she returned to jail, the sentence, under Tennessee law, for a third possession rap, would be a minimum of one year, a felony this time, not a misdemeanor.

I explained to Renae that there was nothing she or I could do to influence the judge, that only God was capable of doing that. Actually, I knew there was something we could do but in order for that to happen, Renae and I would have to have a face-to-face meeting. I asked her if she would meet me tomorrow at noon. She said she would be at work at that time and didn't want to put her job at risk. I said okay, how about tonight at 6:00 at McDonald's in Clarksville. She said that would be good. The meeting was on.

My dog, Oscar, was begging for a good run, so I reversed my earlier plans not to run today. I said, "Oscar, you old four-legged tramp, let's go, but only two miles. You hear me?" He barked his approval and headed for the door. It was another flawless and superb fall day. If the air was any sharper or more quickening, I doubt I'd be able to choke it down. I didn't run toward the river this time. Instead, I followed an old wagon trail west towards highway 48 which is the principal feeder highway into Clarksville from the south.

Clarksville Tennessee was originally a trading center. Tobacco was the commodity being traded the most. River travel and early railroads helped build up the town prior to the Civil War. The aftermath of the war meant hard times all over the south. Clarksville was no exception.

Forward seventy-five years to the bombing of Pearl Harbor by the Japanese. That's when construction began at Fort Campbell, home to the 101st Airborne Division. The base straddles the Kentucky/Tennessee state line and is responsible for a great deal of the Clarksville economy.

Austin Peay State University, where I coached basketball, started as a Masonic Male Academy around 1845. It's been through many changes to get it where it is today – a modern, thriving university. My time coaching there was one of the thrills of my life. I often tell people that when I go to heaven, I'll be excited to see they've got a basketball court up there and that just maybe, I'll be able to play a little one on one with Jesus. I'm not joking. I think that's the way it'll go down. Oh, I know, He will clean my clock really good. But that's not the point. Can you imagine playing ball with The Lord?

So, anyway, Oscar and I ran our two miles and I got myself cleaned up and dressed for the rest of the day, including the 6:30 appointment with Renae Holsclaw. I chose a light blue oxford shirt and tan slacks with a decent leather dress belt, not one of my ratty, old, work belts. I didn't know what a Christian counselor was supposed to look like, so I was simply making the attempt to appear in what I've heard described as "business casual", no tie, no jacket.

I worked at my desk for about an hour, thinking through some of the contingencies I felt were sure to arise in this new Christian counseling I was launching. I quickly scratched off of my worry list the thing I told my son I would look into – professional malpractice and the liability I might be exposed to. I was going to type up a release of liability form that I would have prospective clients sign off on, but I decided against it. Instead, I adopted the reasoning that surely God would not lead me into such a mud hole. As I sat there thinking about it, I made a decision that I felt would allow me to work independently and totally free of any fears of potential liability lawsuits. At the very outset of any counseling relationship, I would tell the client that my methodology was going to be purely spiritual, purely based on both of our understanding that the one Almighty Christian God is sovereign in all things, that His wisdom is sufficient for the problems the client may be facing, that we both will do our best to honor and adhere to the instructions He might give us and finally, that our handshake will be the ultimate binding gesture of non-culpability when it comes to liability. Hey, I know, that's a mouthful, but it all boils down to my client and me would place God first in everything we do and we'd leave the rest of the pieces to fall wherever they may fall. Also, I'd let the client know that if they didn't agree with those ground rules, well then, we'd best pull away and not start a relationship.

The only other thing I felt would be needed before I met with my first client were business cards. I left the house at 4:30 and was in an Office Depot by 5:00. By 5:45 I had five hundred new business cards that were nearly identical to my classified ad –

Christian Counselling, 615-476-0946.

The only thing I added was my name, Finn Weaver.

I pulled into McDonald's at 5:55, parked, walked in, and scanned the restaurant to see if Renae was already there. I didn't see any single women her age, so I went up to the counter and ordered two coffees and took them back to the most remote table I saw.

She was on time and I knew it was her immediately, because when she came in, she did the same thing I had done – scanned the room as if she were looking for someone. I stood up and waved and she started towards my table.

The young lady coming my way was thin but not skinny. She wore jeans, sneakers, and a simple long-sleeved top. She didn't appear to be wearing make-up and her black hair was sort of trussed up into a loose bundle. I'd say maybe she was a plain Jane, but she wasn't. She carried an air of quiet dignity, somehow remaining humble. I wondered if her two previous jail stints had anything to do with the humility.

I was still standing, and tried to give a warm smile, "Hello Renae."

She said, "Coach Weaver." I motioned for her to take a seat and she did.

"I got you a cup of coffee."

"Thanks," and she added cream and sugar and commenced to stir it in.

"Well, here we are," I said. "There are some things I'd like to say before we get started, but first, you. Is there something you want to say or ask?"

"No, not really. I told you most of it on the phone." She looked around the room, I thought maybe to see if anyone could overhear us, but there weren't any people close to us.

"Okay. So, here's the way I'd like to operate, and I want to make sure you agree with the ground rules. You know, I said on the phone that you and I would not be able to influence the judge on the sentencing decision he'll make in your case. Remember?"

"Yes sir."

17

"The truth is there *are* a couple of things we can do and it starts with our total and complete faith and confidence that Jesus Christ, our Lord and Savior, will be in control of the entire situation and see it through to the only possible correct conclusion that there can be – His will be done, not ours. You with me so far? You good with it?"

"Sure," she said, but it was only lukewarm, tepid. It didn't make it to room temperature. I wasn't sure she was buying into the "God model" of the counseling technique I intended to use. As I would later come to understand, it wasn't that she wasn't buying into the "God model", it was more that she didn't totally understand what it meant to give up your will, give it up completely to God. My life experience of sixty-eight years had taught me a lot about what it really means to "let go and let God". I wasn't sure Renae's twenty-five years had taught her the same thing, but I wasn't about to launch an evangelizing lecture at her. I was here to help her. I'd leave it to God to mold her heart the way He wanted it.

I had that thought in mind when I asked her to give me her hand. "Renae, I'm going to pray for us. Let's bow our heads." She did. "Our Heavenly Father, we thank You for this day and we thank You for bringing us together so we might approach You in our desire to help Renae with her problems. Lead us, guide us, direct us, Father. Show us how to overcome these obstacles Renae is facing in order to keep her child. And Father, we ask that You strengthen Renae's heart and pour Your love down on her and her daughter. Show us and teach us, Father, that "Your will be done" is what we need and what we seek, and that it will be more than sufficient. In Jesus name we pray. Amen."

Renae looked up and I believe that her eyes were asking, "What do we do if the prayers don't work?" And I believed she was saying silently, "I can't lose my daughter. I love her so much. I can't let the state take her away."

I believe I read both signals correctly and I was beginning to sense that Renae may be very talkative on the phone, but in person she was much more cautious and unassertive.

"Look, we'll get through this, no matter what happens. I said there are a few things we can do. First, I'll be a character witness, and second, I'll see if I can get the District Attorney on our side. I've known him going back a ways. What's more important is, he knows me. I'll see if maybe he can put in a good word for us to the judge."

"Okay, that sounds good, but it's the same judge that put me away the last two times. I'm afraid he'll really throw away the key this time."

"We can't think like that. Here's the thing. I won't be able to convince the D.A. you've changed, and he won't be able to get the judge's ear, unless you can convince me you have changed."

"What do you mean?"

"Your dope smoking. You're not still using weed are you?"

"No, I quit."

"How long ago?"

"Since the last time I went to jail."

I thought about the timing. "But you've just recently been convicted of possession."

She was quick to respond. "Yeah, but I was just holding a bag for a friend. You asked when I quit smoking."

Oh boy! I thought. "Is that what you told the judge?'

"Yes, it's the truth."

"Renae, I'm not sure the judge's sense of humor matches yours." The problem was, she wasn't trying to be funny.

CHAPTER 3

When I got home that evening, there were two voice mail messages on my smartphone. I'd had the ringer turned off while meeting with Renae. Both callers asked about the ad for Christian Counselling. One of them simply wanted clarification on an important section of scripture from the Bible. I was very familiar with that particular scriptural theme – once saved, always saved. I gave the caller my interpretation and that seemed to be very helpful.

The second call completely blind-sided me. A middle-aged man said he was ready to murder his wife and her secret lover. He said he'd just found out about the adulterous affair and that he was loading his gun as he was speaking.

"No! No!" I shouted into the phone, "Where are you?"

"I'm at my house."

"Where? I'll be right there. Let's talk this out. You can't take two people's lives; I don't care what they've done."

"You watch me."

I sensed that he was one hundred percent for real. He was believable. I didn't feel like this was an idle threat, or, you know, like maybe he only called me to gather a little pity from a third party, or maybe justification for the murders he was about to commit. It was a long shot, but I thought maybe I ought to call his bluff. "Okay, go ahead and kill them, but I've got one question for you."

"What's that?"

"Why did you call me? I'm a counselor. I'm supposed to help you make important decisions, but it looks like you've already made up your mind. Why did you call me?"

"I don't know."

"I know why."

"Why?"

"Because you don't really want to kill them. God had you call me because He knows it also."

"There is no God. Not after this."

"Oh yes there is. I can prove it. Where are you at? What's your address? I'll be right there." He surprised me. He gave me his address.

I thought maybe I had better call the police, but I didn't. Instead, I jumped in my car, put the address he gave me in the GPS, and followed the route to a little north of Clarksville. He lived in Oak Grove, Kentucky. It is just a couple of miles north of the state line. The town sits on the main highway skirting Fort Campbell. His house was what a realtor might describe as "custom contemporary". It had elements of both ranch styled homes and also country estates, but with sharper lines, larger windows, and lots of glass. The house was in the middle of an upper middle-class development, not really a subdivision, because the acreage went anywhere from a full acre up to three acres. I'm pretty good at acreage because my wife had been in real estate.

I parked in the driveway, walked up to the front door, and rang the doorbell. Porch lights came on, but nobody came to the door. It was an hour and a half after dark. I knocked this time. Nothing happened. I knocked again. Still nothing. I opened my phone and called the number the man had used to call me. There was a voicemail message waiting for me: "Counsellor, I changed my mind. It's too late. Don't come over here." I tried to open the front door, but it was locked. I hustled around the side of the house and went around back. There was a deck and I had to be careful climbing the steps because the only light was coming from inside the house through some windows and the big sliding glass door. It was not locked, so I went in the house. Where I entered was the open kitchen area which fed into a dining area and then a large high vaulted ceiling living area. I saw a man sitting way across the other side of the room. He was in a lazy boy, but his feet weren't propped up; they were on the floor. When he saw me, he put the pistol in his hand up to the side of his head. I was thinking that my Christian Counselling Service needed a name. I had no clue as to why that thought arrived in my head or where it had come from. Several names flew across the screen somewhere behind my eyes, "Jonah and the Trail", "Needless Intervention", "Almost Whim", and then the last one, "Beyond Time, Before Creation."

Before any more potential names flittered in, the man in the lazy boy said, "Don't come any closer. I'll do it."

I raised my hands as if there was an invisible wall indicating I would not proceed any further. My Bible was in my left hand. I said, "I got your message. You said you'd changed your mind and it's too late. And you said not to come over here. I didn't get it until just a minute ago. I was on your front porch. You've got a nice house. Did you hear me knock?"

"You can go now."

I put my arms down but I didn't move closer to him. I just stood right there where I was. "I bet you don't remember me. My name is Finnegan Weaver. Everybody calls me Finn. I used to coach basketball over at Austin Peay. Before that, I coached high school, junior high, AAU, and recreation leagues, and way before all of that I even coached Navy teams in an Armed Forces League in Hawaii. You know what's one of the craziest things I've learned after all those years of coaching? Sometimes I think I did my players a lot more harm than good. It was nuts. I remember eighth-grade teams I had. Those kids wanted to please you so much, they'd do anything you told them to do. They'd do it to perfection. I remember one game, we were ahead by a point, one point, and there was only twenty seconds left in the game. It was time-out and I told my kids when the other team brought the ball up the court, to drop back into a tight zone, drop back tight around the basket, don't let them get a shot off close to the bucket. Don't worry about the outside. They did exactly what I asked them to do. They followed my instructions to the letter and lost the game. The other team's best shooter nailed a twenty-footer from where I told my team not to worry about.

"Things like that used to happen all the time. I learned that many times, heck, most of the time, you were better off to let them make their own decisions. I think they actually had a better feel for the game than most coaches. Give them freedom to listen to their inner voice, and I think they invariably made good decisions."

By now he had removed the pistol from the side of his head, but it was still in his hand. Neither one of us said anything. Somewhere around the neighborhood of thirty seconds bled away, and I started talking again. A lot of people said I could talk for a long time without really saying very much.

"I remember another game when I was coaching at Austin Peay. We were on the road at Southern Illinois. This time *we* were down by one, there were sixteen seconds left, and I called time out and had my team huddled up on the sidelines in front of our bench. We had possession under their basket, so, of course, we had to inbound it and bring it up the court and get a shot off. I looked at Charley Sheppard, our point guard, and told him I wanted him to keep the ball in his possession, you know, maintain his dribble up until six seconds to go, and then take the shot. I told him I didn't care whether he made it or not, just as long as he put the ball up on the rim. Then I told my two best rebounders that I wanted them under the basket, one on each side of the lane. Their only job was to get the rebound and put up a lay-up before the buzzer went off. Everybody followed my instructions to the "T", and we won at the buzzer."

The man in the chair moved around a little and looked over at me. "I saw that game on TV."

"Really? You know what? We didn't win it by any great basketball strategy I laid on my players. No sir, that had nothing to do with it. Every game any of my teams ever won was because God was in total control. And I don't mean He plays favorites. I don't believe He sways the outcomes of games to a team that's "more Christian" than another team. I've never believed that to be the case. But I do believe that's the way to success in life. I don't worry about wins and losses. All I try to do is to learn from each experience that God gives me.

Sometimes His wisdom comes with pain and anguish. Sometimes it's pure joy. When we learn lessons from God, we're better for it. We're better men. I can see now that even the hardest lessons in my life were put there for a reason."

I stopped for a few seconds and then I asked him, "Do you have any coffee?"

He put the gun down, got up, and walked over near me and he said, "I never saw it coming." He went on back into the kitchen and popped two of those little coffee pouches into his Keurig, and we had hot coffee in 20 seconds. He placed both cups on a small table and sat down. I sat across from him. "I mean it's not like we've had a perfect marriage, God knows. But *this*, I never … I mean *never* had a clue she was doing this to me."

"You ever play much basketball?"

"Just pick-up games," he said.

"I was on a Navy team out in Hawaii. I was twenty years old. It was a tough Armed Forces League – Army, Navy, Marines, Air Force, and a couple of civilian teams with mostly ex-college players. A lot of good ball players. Our team had some talent, but nothing like the other teams. The two years I was on that team we had not won a single game. About halfway through that second year my teammates and I made a decision that we had to get a new coach. We felt like it was his fault we were losing. I don't remember why, but my teammates decided that I should be the guy to tell our coach we no longer wanted to play for him. Can you imagine? Hey coach, we're throwing you under the bus. And I was the guy chosen to deliver the message. I did it, but I wasn't happy about it. The poor guy was a young lieutenant in charge of special services for our Navy base. It tore him up when I told him."

"What are you saying?"

"I'm not sure. Maybe it's this: Sometimes we get loads dropped on us, and like you said, we never see it coming. When it hits us, it's too late. There's nothing we can do about it. We're like a worm squashed in the dirt. It looks like the only thing we can do is wiggle around until we die. So, think about that young lieutenant. It must have felt like his own children were disowning him. And even me, the guy that broke the bad news to him. I wasn't the same for a long time."

We were quiet for a while, but I'm sure you can guess who started up again. "It's really pretty simple. Once the load is dropped on us, it's too late. You gotta' agree with me on that, right?" He didn't say anything. "Hey, the only thing we can do to make it through this life is to be prepared ahead of time. We need to be ready for the assaults, the bombs, the misfortunes, the misery that is sure to target us. We need to have a defensive wall built around us before these evils strike. If we don't, we may find ourselves in the same place you were in five minutes ago."

"I'm still in that place."

"No, you're not. You're sitting at a table with me, drinking a cup of coffee." Again, he didn't say anything. "By the way, that reminds me. If I'm going to continue being your counselor, I'm making a rule. I'd like to do at least one session a week out at my place. There are some nice spots down by the river. Can you make it at nine tomorrow morning?" I put directions on my card, pushed the card across the table towards him, and got up and left.

CHAPTER 4

I was up at 5:30 the next morning, a little early for me, but I wasn't sleeping anyway. After I went outside for my morning expulsions, I came back in and put a fire in the woodstove. It was a cool, crisp morning, temps in the mid-forties. While the coffee was brewing, I went to my knees in prayer. It didn't take long. Usually, my prayers tend to be compact. Truth be known, I'm praying all day long. Little ones here and there, about this and that. I guess you might say I've got addicted to praying. Thinking about it, I realized I was engaging in the activity I introduced to the man at his house last night – building defensive perimeters around me *before* the you know what hits the fan.

Shirley, my cat, was whining and crying for attention. I knew what she wanted – for me to sit down in the big comfort recliner so she could curl up on my lap. It didn't happen. And that's when Oscar, my black Lab, started demanding we go on a three-mile run together. That didn't happen either, but I did let him out of the house – let him run all he wanted to. Sir Winston Churchill once said, "I like pigs. Dogs look up to us. Cats look down on us. Pigs treat us as equals." You gotta love ol' Sir Winston. He must have been cut from the same cloth as W.C. Fields.

I made breakfast – an apple, an orange, a banana, and oatmeal. I watched the morning news on the tube and then I went to my desk and began reviewing the few notes I had taken on my first Christian counseling adventure:

Renae Holsclaw, twenty-five, third MJ possession – could lose daughter to state custody. Need to call Rod Templeton, D.A.

I waited until 8:15 and called the D.A.'s office. A secretary answered. "Rod Templeton's office. How may I help you?"

"Good morning, this is Finn Weaver. I'd like to speak with Rod, please."

"Coach Weaver? Sure. I think he's free. Hold just a second."

I'd known Rod Templeton for about twenty years. One of his sons had been a backup small-forward on one of my teams at Austin Peay. The kid's name was Pepper. He was about six-six and he weighed in around one-eighty-five, a little on the thin side. He had a good outside shot and that's what I used him for – a three-point bomber, a zone-buster.

Rod's no-nonsense D.A. voice charged through the line, "Rod Templeton." He sounded like he didn't have any time for small talk.

"Good morning, Rod, … Finn Weaver."

"Coach Weaver, good morning, what can I do for you?"

"Squeeze me in for lunch in the next day or two, my treat. There's something I need to talk to you about."

"Can't make it today, how about tomorrow?"

"Great. Let's say 12:30. Meet you at Cindy's. Will that work for you?"

"Sure, 12:30 at Cindy's. See you then."

So, now that I had an appointment with the D.A., an appointment concerning Renae Holsclaw, I realized I'd better turn my focus to the man from last night. Would he show up at nine this morning? And what was I going to say to him if he did? I realized I didn't even know his name. First, he'd told me he was going to "murder" his wife and her secret lover and then when I went into his house, he put a gun to his head and said "Don't come any closer. I'll do it." What kind of a man was I dealing with? What could I do in a situation so full of potentially explosive energy, emotions so raw they could fly out of control in a heartbeat? I knew there was nothing I could do. Nothing at all. But I knew who could do something. Sure could. Does it all the time. The question was, could I get past the man's pain, misery, and distress and either introduce him to The Healer or reintroduce him in the event he'd known Him earlier but had lost touch? I went to my knees in prayer, and it must have been one of my lengthier pursuits because it seemed to go on and on. Then I heard a car pull up outside and a knock at my door.

I got up, walked over, opened the door and there he was – the man from last night. He showed up, but he was not alone. He had a woman with him. "Come in, come in," I said.

"No, we'd better not. You said last night something about the river."

"Sure ... uh, let me get a couple of things. I'll be right out." I had no idea what was going on, other than, of course, I did remember telling him there were some nice places down on the river. Hey, if that's what the Big Man upstairs wanted, then that's where we'd start sorting things out. I filled a thermos with coffee, grabbed a bag of donuts, threw on a light jacket, grabbed the keys to my old pick-up truck and headed out the door. They were both standing there on the walkway.

I said, "Hold on a minute. I forgot something." I went back inside, picked up my Bible, and hustled back outside.

"We'll drive down in the truck," I said and opened up the door on the passenger side. The man nudged the woman in first, he followed, and I closed the door. I got in on my side and started the truck. The woman looked to be about the same age as the man. I'd say late forties, but she certainly was showing the worse for wear. I mean, I could see she could be an attractive woman when she had the opportunity, but this morning wasn't one of those times. She must have been crying very hard for I don't know how long. Her eyes were red and puffy, and her entire presence seemed stretched to the limit. She was hurting. She kept her eyes down, not interested in our drive through the woods. He didn't look all that much better, but I don't think he'd been crying.

When I wangled the truck out of my gravel driveway, I aimed it at the opening to an old wagon trail and we bumped along towards the river about a half mile away. I stopped the truck and we all got out. The cold, gray Cumberland River was rolling by way down below us. The high banks we were perched on were a hundred and fifty feet above the river's sharp turn to the west that endless seasons had chiseled out of the earth's rocky crust. It was a beautiful spot that I visited every now and then. A quarter mile across the river you could see low rolling bottom-land etched with line after line, acre after acre of dried cornstalks, all destined for silage. Beyond that, the colors of fall emblazoned the slowly rising hills which in another

32

hundred miles would become the western slopes of the Appalachian Mountains. Locals called such a spot that we were at a "bluff" and this one had a name – Perkin's Bluff. It was named after a hapless lady of the 1830's. Her man had caught her in a forbidden tryst and thrown her into the frigid, unwelcoming river below. I didn't plan on relating this history to my two companions and for a brief moment I thought about moving on to someplace else. I didn't. I felt like this was the place we were supposed to be.

Nobody had spoken a word on the way to Perkin's Bluff, and as I quickly built a fire at the little camp site, still, no one was ready to start talking. I surprised myself. I surely did but thought it best to let these two open up on their own. I motioned them to a couple of rough camp chairs near the fire and placed paper cups in their hands and then poured them both some hot coffee. I got myself a cup, put the bag of donuts on the ground between them, and finally sat on the butt of a log maybe ten feet from them but at an angle where we had a good visual line of sight.

What would happen next? I didn't know. It was all in God's hands.

"This is a nice place," the man said.

"Thanks. It's not mine, It's my neighbors land."

He looked like he wanted to say more and after a couple of minutes of silence, he finally started talking. I noticed that during the two minutes the woman had kept her head down and she'd been weeping the whole time. You'd see her wiping away tears with her hands.

"I'm Justin Barkley. This is my wife, Julie."

That's all it took. The woman, Julie, erupted with the most tormented, hurtful outcry I had ever witnessed. Her grief was overwhelming. It was palpable in my own bones. Oh, what pain she must have been experiencing. I had never seen anything like it, at funerals, accidents, extreme loss, you name it. I'd never seen anything like this before.

We both let her go through it, get it out. We let her navigate that deserted, desolate, destitute trail all by herself – that trail that only the very most lonely could recognize. It took a while, but she got through it. Her howling dropped off to simple crying and then to sniffling and whimpering as if she couldn't quite catch her breath. Finally, Mr. Perkins put his arm around her shoulders, and I walked over and did the same.

"Julie, it's going to be okay. You're going to be okay. Justin is going to be okay." I said it with all the confidence I could put into it.

"No, it's not." She threw it back at me hard and I thought maybe we were heading down sob street again. But you got to hand it to her. She was keeping it together.

"Look," I said. "This may not be easy, but now that we've got this far – you're here, Justin is here, and I'm here – now we've got this far, let's just see how far we can go. Does that sound okay? If you tell me to stop, I'll stop. Okay?"

She mumbled something I didn't catch. It was like her voice, her vocal cords, were incapable of responding to the purpose and will of her brain. But she said something. It was weak and tiny. I said a quick internal prayer, actually it was a question I posed to the Lord: "What was it she said, Lord?"

SHE SAID, "Go on. Proceed."

Proceed I did. "I'm going to ask both of you a question. It's a simple question, but I'd like for you to really think about it. There's no hurry. It's the same question for each one of you.

Have you ever in your life asked Jesus Christ to be your personal Savior, to take control of everything you do?

"Now, while you're thinking about that one, I've got another question for you. The day you got married, did the preacher say something like this, 'put this marriage in God's hands. If you do, it will be a successful marriage.' And, if the preacher did say words to that effect, is that what you did?"

The questions didn't seem to shock or surprise Justin. Julie, on the other hand, appeared to slide backwards, right back down that dark, lonely tunnel I was hoping she might have crawled out of. She was crying again, and waves of spasmodic emotion were raking her over the black volcanic rock of her recent folly and indiscretion. I was thinking I might lose her.

"Julie, I know you've been through a lot. Nobody, me or anyone else could understand what you may be feeling right now. But I know another woman that something very similar happened to."

"You do?" she asked. *Thank God* I was thinking. I could hear her words this time.

"I certainly do. You want to know what it was?"

"I don't think it would be the same."

"You're right, it's not the same, but the underlying principle is exactly the same. Don't you want to hear it?"

"I don't know. I guess you want to tell me, don't you?"

"I sure do."

"Okay," Julie said. I saw her drying a few tears.

"Julie, how long have you been married to Justin?"

"Twenty-five years."

"Once, Julie, there was a woman who had had five different husbands in her past, and she was currently living with a man who was not her husband. In that part of the world, Julie, and in that time, those kinds of living arrangements were strictly forbidden. She was going about her business one day and a complete stranger, a man she had never seen before, asked her for a drink of water. She was surprised because she was from a downtrodden part of that particular area, you might say a minority, but the strange man was obviously from a higher class of people." I paused and looked right at Julie, "You with me so far?"

"I think so."

"Good, what happens next is that the man who asked the lowly woman for a drink of water says that if she knew who he truly was that the question would have been reversed – she would have asked him for a drink of water. Sounds crazy, huh?"

"I guess so. I don't get it."

"Julie, it's all about who this man really was. He tells her that if she *had* asked him for a drink of water, he would have given her *living water*."

"I still don't get it."

"You've never heard the story before?"

"No."

"Okay, you know what?"

"No."

"I'm going to change what I told you before. Remember, I said nobody could understand what you may be feeling. Well, I'm changing my tune. Now I think maybe I understand. Julie, who do you think the man was, the man who said he would have given the lowly woman *living water*?"

"I don't know."

"It was Jesus Christ."

"Aw. Come on … You gonna' throw the Bible at me?" She seemed genuinely betrayed.

"Julie, you and the woman in the Bible had never been confronted straight on with the truth of Jesus Christ, Am I right? Tell me if I'm wrong. But then she met him face to face, and today you've met Him spirit to spirit. In the same Bible scripture this story is taken from, Jesus, in fact, tells us that God *is* spirit. Guess what that means?" She had no idea what I was talking about, but I noticed her sniffling and weeping had nearly ended.

"Let me back up just a bit. Jesus also told the woman that whoever drinks regular water will continue to get thirsty. Now, Julie, you have to admit, that makes sense, doesn't it?"

She glanced my way with a look of bland indifference, but she didn't say anything. I said, "Jesus continued – but whoever drinks the water I give him will never get thirsty. The water I give will become a fountain of water springing up into everlasting life. The woman says, okay, give me this water. Jesus says go get your husband. The woman says I don't have one. No, you don't, says Jesus, but you've had five and now you're living with a man who is not your husband."

I looked at Julie and saw something change in her face and I figured this was a sign to continue. "Julie, you and the woman, both of you have been confronted by Jesus. None of us is perfect, we all make mistakes, we all sin. Jesus knew all about the woman's history, and He knows all about yours. He told the woman about the living water becoming a fountain of water springing up into everlasting life. And He's telling you the same thing. You talk to Him, Julie. You could tell him about the mistakes you've made, but He already knows. He's ready to forgive you, Julie. Just talk to Him. Trust Him. He'll show you a way to deal with this mess you are in. It will be His way, not your way. His way will work, Julie. Trust me; it's the best way, the only way."

"Are you a preacher?" Julie asked me.

"No, I'm just a sinner, but I've got some new spiritual territory to explore." I wasn't sure she was with me on that, but I didn't see any more tears.

CHAPTER 5

The next morning, I awoke to the questionable sensation of Oscar's fat, slobbery tongue slapping against my feet and toes. He had pulled the cover off half of the bed, jumped up, and started licking and nibbling on my feet. It was his way of saying, "Come on Finn. Let's go for a run." I agreed with him. A good, aggressively paced four-miler was the correct way to start a new day.

It took a while for me to get dressed, put the coffee on, and attend to other early morning necessities. When we finally got started, we headed off down the same trail I had taken the Barkleys on yesterday to Perkin's Bluff. Oscar didn't do a very good job of staying on the trail. Most of the time he was off in the woods chasing gray squirrels back up the trees they had jumped down from. The trail came to a Y. Right would take me to Perkin's Bluff. Left swung way back around the other way, eventually taking me to a quarter mile behind my property line. I went right.

When I got to the spot where the campfire had been, I stopped running and walked all around the area. The two camp chairs the Barkleys had sat in were still there just a few feet from the burnt-out area where I had built the fire. I walked the forty-five feet over to where the cliffs at the top of the bluff actually fell off to the river a hundred and fifty feet below. I thought back to what happened yesterday. I couldn't believe she would do it – jump off the cliff. After she had asked me if I was a preacher and I said, "No, I'm just a sinner," after that, I said to both of them that I was going out in the woods for a few minutes. You see, I was feeling like now was the time to get out of the way, that now was the time to let them be together, alone. Lord have mercy, how wrong I was. I stayed out there in the woods at least ten minutes and then I felt like that was enough time. I started back in towards the bluff. I must have gotten back within forty feet from where they were, but they couldn't see me. They weren't in the chairs, no, they were standing up, sort of face to face, definitely in a confrontational posture. They were arguing, very loud, very aggressive. I saw Justin Barkley back off and turn to walk away. That's when she lit out for the cliff. She was slow at first, just a few steps in that direction. I was already on the move. I didn't like the looks of this. Then, she picked up her pace and jumped into a dead sprint. By the time I came out of the woods she was about twenty-five feet from the cliff, and I was ten feet behind her. She was going to go over. I wouldn't reach her in time. I don't know where it came from, well, I guess actually I do. A mega shot of adrenaline jerked through my arteries, and I must have made three or four strides in half the time I normally would. But that wasn't going to save her.

What saved her was the low branch coming off that same log I had been sitting on. It caught the tip of my toe and sent me off into a swan dive. I could see her feet leaving the ground, nothing in front of her but sky and nothing below her but river. As I was falling through the air, I lurched my arms out as far as I could, you know, like a wide receiver stretching for a hail Mary in the end zone. I snagged her left ankle, just barely. It was a good thing she wasn't a large woman. If she had been, I never could have held on, or, I guess, she might have dragged me over with her.

By now, of course, Justin was aware of Julies intentions, and he helped me reel her back in. He had managed to grasp her right foot. It wasn't easy. She was trying to kick both of us off. She finally wore out, and we drug her up, up over the edge, back to safety.

Justin was holding her in case she wanted to jump again, and I started in on her with a fervor that shocked even me, "Julie, listen to me! Listen to me! I can prove it. I can prove that God will forgive you. Just give me a chance. Please, just give me a chance." I really did know that I could prove it. I also knew that I couldn't prove it if she had sailed over that cliff. Justin was talking to her as we lifted her to her feet. "Baby, please don't, please don't ... I couldn't ..." He couldn't go on is probably what he had intended to say, but he never finished it.

I said, "Let's get her into the truck." We could see some of the damage she had done to herself as we walked her back to the truck. She was scratched up and battered pretty good from when she had slammed back against the rocks when I caught her ankle.

We drove back to my house and this time they accepted my invitation to come inside. We put her on the sofa, and Justin dropped down beside her. I went to the bathroom and came back quickly with wet wash cloths, dry towels, and some hydrogen peroxide. Justin started cleaning her up, and I brought her a glass of water. She drank a little water, and we all just sat there not saying anything. Then the crying started again, but this time it wasn't Julie, it was Justin.

That told me something.

"Okay guys, I've tried to keep a neutral stance, and like Justin told me last night, your marriage hasn't been the perfect marriage; you know, the warm and fuzzy Cinderella love story. Maybe it was at one time. Guess what? Those kinds of marriages are more rare than pineapples growing at the North Pole. And I'd bet you everything I own that the problems in your marriage are not one sided. I'd bet you in a New York minute there's plenty of blame to pass around to everybody." I noticed Justin flinching like maybe somebody was pelting him with a BB gun. But I knew where I was going, and I knew it was time to get there. Past time.

"I asked you both two questions earlier. Somehow, we never answered those questions. Well, maybe a little with Julie, but not so much with Justin, Now … I have a question for you Justin. Do you remember last night we were on the phone, and I asked you why you called me? Remember that?"

"Uh, yeah, I remember." He was still crying softly.

"Okay, good. Do you remember your answer?"

"I said I didn't know why I called you."

"Right, and I said you called because God didn't want you to kill Julie and another man. Am I right? Is that what I said?"

42

"I guess so. Yeah, that's what you said." Julie seemed to be surprised by that and she shrank a little, into a pale cloud.

"Okay guys, we're getting close to it now. Bear with me. The real reason Justin called me instead of the other counselling listings is one word – Christian. He saw that word and called me, not the other counselors who don't have that word in their ad. It was that one word that kept him from going out last night and killing two people, kept him from committing suicide, and kept Julie from doing the same. I bet neither of you know that I'm brand-new at this counselling game. That's right, you are only my second case. My first case is a young lady who is trying desperately to maintain custody of her little baby girl. She may be going away for some serious time because of her third drug possession violation. I'm brand new at counselling, but I'm not brand new at life. You see, I know that God can fix your marriage. And I know that you're both in so much pain right now that that very idea seems lame, maybe even trite, a false promise I'm trying to get you to bite into. Is that what is sounds like to you?" They just sat there. Didn't say anything.

"So, back to the questions I asked you up on the bluff. Have you ever given your hearts to Jesus? Your marriage?"

Like so many people, the question to Julie and Justin, would be answered quickly and falsely with something like, "Oh sure. I believe in God," or "Yeah, we go to church," or (this is the one that really gets me) "Jesus, of course. He was a great teacher of love, a great prophet." Julie and Justin were no different. Their eyes and their words had all three of those typical responses. I won't re-tell them here. This is what I said to them:

"Julie, Justin, we have now arrived. We are at the place I'm sure neither one of you wanted to be. We are at the place of truth. And here is the truth. You both have never cared enough about your marriage to place it in God's hands. Why? Because neither one of you has ever asked Jesus Christ to be Lord of your life. You can't have God The Father in control of your marriage if you don't have His Son in control of your heart. Unless you accept His suffering, bleeding, and death on the cross as the one and only sacrifice that He made for you that is capable of forgiving all of your sins, then not only your marriage, but your entire life will be unsuccessful. That's the bad news – the truth. Here's the good news, also the truth. The pain, anguish, suffering, torment, shame, and guilt ... all of that will go away if you truly accept Jesus into your heart. It can happen today; it can happen right now. All you have to do is to want Jesus to take on all that baggage that is killing both of you. That's why God The Father sent Him, to do that very thing. But you have to *want* Him. You must *want* Him to take control. I can quote scripture all day long that will verify what I've said is the truth. But in the end, it all comes down to one simple act. You must ask Jesus into your heart. That's all you have to do. You must mean it. If you do, your life will change, you'll be born again, and yes, your marriage will be a beautiful thing. You can make it happen. It's up to you.   Think about it together. Talk it over, together. I'll be back in ten minutes."

I left the room and went outside to look for Oscar. I found him running and sniffing around the edge of the woods with a dog from up the road. It was one of my neighbor's dogs, He was an American Bulldog, big, solid white and as loveable as any dog you'd ever see. The neighbors called him Casper. While the dogs frolicked and acted like dogs, I prayed and acted like Finnegan Weaver. In other words, I put all my faith and confidence in the fact that God would take control of the situation with Julie and Justin – that His will would be done. In my mind that's what Christian counselling was all about – praying for God's will to be done.

When I went back inside, I found them sitting there together like two children. They weren't children, but that's what it felt like when I saw them.

It was Julie, "We'd like to try it. You know, asking Jesus to be Lord of our life."

Justin said, "That's right. We want to try it, but we don't know how to … uh, how to, you know, how to ask Him."

"Any way you do it will work, as long as you mean it, as long as you truly want Him in your hearts. When I did it, forty years ago, I said four words. That's all I did, but I had never in my life wanted anything more than I wanted what was in those four words."

They looked at me doubtfully, but then Julie asked, "What were the four words?"

"Jesus please take me," I said.

That was all the day before. The next day, I had a meeting with the Montgomery County D. A., Rod Templeton. I had two new messages on my cell phone. They were both asking about my Christian Counselling Service. One was from a grandmother who was concerned about her grandson's recent enlistment into the Marines. The other call was very strange, very weird. I could not begin to break it down to anything intelligible. I would put it out of my mind until later in the afternoon. Maybe by then a path forward on Renae Holsclaw's case would begin to appear.

I sat down at my desk and was thinking about the last four days, and I was thinking about any additional steps I would need to take in order for my Christian Counselling Service to thrive. Already, I could see there was one step I would not need to take – setting up a web site to attract clients. The ads in the two newspapers were working, I thought, very well. Already I was averaging two or three calls a day. It was beginning to look like many of the people who were calling would be able to be serviced to their satisfaction just by a counselling session or two on the phone. Obviously, not all cases could be handled that easily. Two cases in point: Justin and Julie Barkley, and Renae Holsclaw. Would I ever get another case similar to the Barkleys? I had no idea. Time would tell. This was God's counselling service, not mine. I was just volunteer help.

I set out for Cindy's Diner to meet Rod Templeton at 12:30. Cindy's was a favorite of city workers and Austin Peay staff. I knew I would see a lot of my old coaching chums when I walked in as well as police and courthouse people. As usual, Cindy's was packed and there was Rod Templeton just inside the entrance. Three others had surrounded him, each one trying to get his ear on some compelling legal issue, or maybe an important upcoming case. Rod saw me come in, broke away from the folks pressing him, and we headed off for the farthest corner we could find. We found a table and Rod started off, "It's already been a busy day and it's only 12:30. You saw those three up at the door? You know what they wanted, don't you? Who am I going to endorse in the Sheriff's race? Don't those idiots know I can't endorse anybody?"

I had a smile on my face, "Well, who *are* you going to endorse?"

"Ferdy Collins." We both laughed. He said, "How've you been, coach? What did you drag me in here for?"

"First, tell me about Pepper. How's he doing?"

"Swell, just swell, as they used to say. Two little girls, a good job down in Memphis. I couldn't be prouder."

"That's great. You remember that Vanderbilt game? I think it was eighteen he put on them – six threes."

"Yeah, those were fun days. You did a good job with that team. What did you want to talk about?"

A waitress came over, "What can I get you Mr. Templeton, Coach Weaver?" We didn't need menus. We both ordered chicken and dumplings, turnip greens and cornbread.

"Rod, I've started a Christian counselling service. I don't charge anything. You know, I'm just trying to help a few people. My very first case, it seems, I think you could help me out."

"Gratis advise, eh? And I'm assuming you have no credentials other than your coaching experience and your reputation."

"That would be correct."

"Let's flip it. My advice to you would be to find some other hobby. The liability exposure would be huge. But knowing you, I'm guessing you've already dismissed any such concerns. Tell me about this first case you have."

I told him everything I knew about Renae Holsclaw and all of the details of her pending sentencing hearing. Of course, I didn't leave out the fact that I wanted him to do whatever he could to let the judge know that I thought the girl was forthright and honest even though her claim of simply "holding" a bag of dope for a friend would rival any absurd and ridiculous defensive statement in the history of Montgomery County's legal system.

We had nearly finished our meal. The last thing the D. A. said to me was, "Finn, I wish you well with your intent to help folks with your counselling program, but I must warn you. Judge Bellows is not the type of judge to place any credence in Miss Holsclaw's outrageous defense. I'll speak to him and convey your thoughts about the veracity of her story, but I don't think you should get your hopes up."

Later that afternoon, when I figured Renae would be home from work, I called her and reported on the D. A.'s icy prediction of the outcome of her sentencing hearing. I could sense her disappointment and the doom which now stalked her. I did my best to keep hope alive, but of course we would just have to wait and see what was going to happen. The hearing was two weeks away.

CHAPTER 6

It was later that evening that I finally took a closer look at that very strange call that had come in. I cued up the message and listened to it again:

The word's getting around. Your counselling is off to a good start. But what if you could help millions of people rather than a tiny handful? Think about it and pay attention to your dreams.

That was the whole message. I played it again and sat back shaking my head. I played it again. Maybe there was something I missed. I played it several more times so I could write it down word for word. I sat there at my desk scratching my head. I looked at it and reread it again and again.

The voice that delivered the message seemed to be a serious, rational male voice. I detected a mountain enunciation and meter. I had recruited some of my players from east Tennessee Appalachia, so I knew what that accent sounds like. Whoever this was had just enough of it that I was sure of where he was from. Other than that, I had no clue who this person was or what he was trying to do. I looked at my phone again and cued the message one more time. I stared at the caller's phone number, 423-777-7777. What? Are you kidding me? That's impossible. The 423 I recognized easily – upper east Tennessee, what they call the tri-cities region – Johnson City, Kingsport, and Bristol. But the 777-7777? God's number seven times. The plausibility of such a phone number didn't seem to me to be reliable. There was only one way to find out. I punched in the return call button and watched my screen. The call was being sent through. It was ringing.

"The number you've called is not in service at this time. Please try your call again later." It wasn't the man's voice. It was one of those succinct, compact female telephone company voices. I was right back where I was earlier that morning. The message was a brain tease. It didn't make any sense. Yet, it possessed inside knowledge as to how my efforts at counselling were progressing. I wracked my brain trying to think of anyone in east Tennessee that could possibly be aware of what I was doing here in middle Tennessee. I quickly dismissed my son Aaron. He lived very close to Knoxville, nearly a hundred miles from area code 423. And it wasn't his voice delivering the message. If I had to guess, I'd say the voice belonged to someone much older than Aaron. Frustration was setting in. But what could I do? I could grill an eighteen-ounce New York Strip and build myself a blue cheese salad and heat up a roll of heavenly artisan bread which I have a spirited fondness for. And that's what I set out to do.

The grill was outside on the deck at the rear of the house. I started that way so I could light the charcoal and hickory chips which were going to sear that steak to perfection. No sir. I didn't need to worry about a prank call which somehow made it through all the cell towers, satellites, and fiber optic cables to my ears. The first thing I noticed when I stepped outside onto

50

the deck were my running shoes. The reason I noticed is because I never leave them out there. I always take them off inside the house when I return from a run and place them in a little stink box. The stink box is an ingenious invention. It deodorizes excessively rank, sour smelling shoes. I bought one of the devices two years ago the instant I saw them come on the market. But my toxic, rank smelling running shoes were not in the stink box, they were outside on the deck. How could that be?

The second brain tease of the evening had now occurred, but I wasn't thinking "what will be next?" I wrote both of these baffling events off as simple unexplainable conundrums, you know – stuff happens. I got the grill fired up and went back inside and began working on the salad, and the bread. Thirty years ago, I would have popped the cork on a bottle of good Cabernet Sauvignon, but not since then. Instead, I filled a tall glass with iced tea. The steak was pretty good, the salad, on a scale of 1 to 10, probably earned a 9, and the bread, after warming up and buttering, came in at 1,000. I ate a good half loaf. Then, a great cup of coffee. I have yet to find any blend better than the Costa Rican Tarrazu. I grabbed a mystery novel I'd been reading and dived into the big comfort chair, my book in one hand and the coffee mug on the table next to me. Oscar and Shirley were both spread out on the floor in front of the woodstove. The perfect picture of an old, single, coach, bathed in the lap of domesticity and comfort. After an hour of reading, I'd be ready for nighty-night. That's when the brain teasers would start up again, this time at warp speed.

I always dreamed a lot, probably more than most people. Sometimes the impetus for my dreams is easy to pinpoint, other times I have no idea what kick starts my dreams. Usually, my dream adventures don't start until very late in the night, many times not until sunrise. But that night they started just after midnight. I'm sure of the timing because I got up after the first dream and looked at the clock. Old men are not uncommon visitors to the bathroom in the middle of the night. I might be a world record holder at two and sometimes three trips a night.

I'm dialing up 423-777-7777. That's how the first dream started. A man's voice in a high crusted, English accent answered the phone with, "Beyond Time, Before Creation, may I help you?"

"Yes," I said, "I'm trying to reach The Heavenly Father. Is He in the office?"

"May I ask what this pertains to?"

I could see pretty much what the English guy looked like. He was sort of a cross between Abe Lincoln and Winston Churchill. He seemed friendly enough and he had a mischievous smile which somehow warmed the soles of my feet. I said, "Why yes, of course. This pertains to my new existence."

"Ah, yes. We've been expecting your call, but I'm afraid the Boss is not here right now. However, He left a message for you that He said is very important."

"Really? He left a message for me?"

"Absolutely. Let me see if I can find it. It was right here a moment ago." I could see the Englishman sailing through some far-off galaxy and suddenly plucking a brilliant star from eternity. He was back in no time flat. He read the message to me:

"*Terry Fox is waiting for you. He's wondering why you haven't started yet?*"

"Uh, I don't get it."

"That's the message He left for you."

"You sure there's nothing else?"

"That's all."

"Say, I was wondering," I said, "Could you tell me why the soles of my feet are warming up?"

"That's for you to determine. You can call us back anytime you have a question."

The dream ended. Just like that, it was over. That's when I got up to go to the bathroom. Knowing that dreams fade quickly, I wanted to retain the message "The Boss" had left for me. Yes, I know, it was just a dream, but my compulsion to hang on to that message was overwhelming. When I got back to my bedroom, I jotted it down on a piece of paper.

As I laid down and pulled the covers up to my chin, I was thinking about that name – Terry Fox. It was very familiar, but I couldn't place it on anybody I knew. I was surprised it didn't keep me awake, but it didn't. I went back to sleep.

The next time I awoke, it was for the same reason as the first time – that burning bladder that demanded the fire be put out, but it was also the maddening torment of my second dream sequence. I looked at the clock again. It was 3:30 and I went back to the bedroom and before lying down, I scribbled some notes that were still ringing in my head from that second dream trip of the night. This time there was no reference to Terry Fox. Instead, I was witness to some kind of historical replay of events from the 1980's. It started with newspaper headlines about "Just Say No" and then the headlines changed to "DARE", and then they went to "MADD". Something about Carrolton, Kentucky showed up, and although I couldn't see what happened, I knew in my heart that many people had died and many more injured. The dream speeded up into a kaleidoscope of activity. There were drugs everywhere, drinking alcohol, runners, mothers with innocent children, wrecks, confusion, chaos and death.

After that second bathroom trip I eventually got back to sleep and the crazed, frenzied nightmare picked up right where it had left off. The pace and scope of havoc, devastation, and desolation I thought might choke me to death – suffocate me. I knew I was dreaming, but I couldn't escape. I wanted it to end. It wouldn't.

I awoke in a cold sweat at sun-up.

I walked around a few minutes in a fog of frustration, anxiety, and questioning. What was going on? Did the older man with the mountain accent not suggest that I pay attention to my dreams? And in my dreams, did "The Boss" not say, "Terry Fox was waiting for me and he's wondering why I haven't started yet?" I was beginning to wonder if the blue cheese I had in my salad last night wasn't tainted with some psycho-active bacterium.

Oscar was wagging his tail standing over by the door leading outside to the deck. When I opened the door for him, I expected him to dash off into the woods. That's not what he did. He put his head down low to the deck and I could see that he was nudging my running shoes with his nose. He'd look up at me and then back to my running shoes. Wait just a minute I said to myself. I had put those shoes back in the stink box last night after I had found them outside on the deck. Another brain tease? Or was somebody, or *some thing* messing with me?

My phone was ringing back in the bedroom. By the time I got back there I'd missed it. There was a message and I couldn't help noticing the return number was 423-777-7777. I was reluctant to hit the play button. I hit it. "Good morning Coach

Finn. How'd you sleep? Say, it looks like Oscar is trying to tell you something. He's a good dog. Smart too." That was it, nothing more. I was ready to pull my hair out. I punched the call-back button and got the same message as before, "The number you've called is not in service at this time."

CHAPTER 7

I had some decisions to make. It was the sixth day since I'd placed the ads for my Christian counselling service. I felt like I'd gotten off to a pretty good start. But now, after last night's bizarre events, dreams, and shoes moving around all by themselves, I found myself asking a not so simple question: Did I really believe that God was in control, or was there something altogether different going on? I had the feeling that the answer to my question was going to determine whether or not I should stay the course on my "new existence" – the Christian counselling – or if I'd be better off to forget the whole idea.

I didn't even have to pray on it. By the time I had a pot of coffee brewed, I knew I was sticking with the first option – God was always in control. I may not understand how, but I understood the notion that I could trust God. My heart could trust God. I knew there was nothing else in this humongous cosmos called eternity that I could trust, like I could trust Him.

That's when I prayed. Oh, I don't know how many hallelujahs, thank yous, and amens I must have thrown upwards to heaven, upwards to God.

But I did know I had some work to do. What were all of these signs supposed to mean – the unexplainable phone calls, the dreams, who was Terry Fox? What about the shoes? What about everything? What was I supposed to do next?

I sat down at my desk with the notes I scribbled from my dreams. The first thing I did was google the name Terry Fox. There were plenty of articles about who he was and what he had done, and it all came back to me. Of course, now I remembered. He was the twenty-two-year-old Canadian who'd lost a leg to a rare cancer and dedicated the rest of his life to cancer research. The first thing he did was to attempt a fund raiser by trying to run over 5,000 miles across the continent on one good leg and one prosthetic leg. He got as far as 3,200 miles before complications of the cancer put him in a hospital. He died six months later. Proceeds from his run and other fund raisers in his name have now exceeded eight hundred million dollars. Many recognize Terry Fox as the greatest Canadian hero ever. Prior to his doomed run, he was a distance runner and a basketball player. Bingo! There it was – the connection that I'd nearly forgotten.

Figuring out his identity didn't answer many of the questions I had, but it was a start. Next, I googled "Just Say No". I remembered what that organization was all about, but I checked it out on my google search, just to make sure. I had it right. The "Just Say No" clubs were an effort by Nancy Reagan to support youth across America to Just Say No to drugs and alcohol. There were various groups and organizations, including the government in the 80's who had continued the war on drugs began by Richard Nixon. The Reagans were both doing all they could to combat illegal drug use in the Unites States. Here in Middle Tennessee, I remember one man who did his best Terry Fox representation by running and walking across the United States to raise money for the Just Say No Foundation. He didn't have cancer nor was he missing a leg. He said he was doing it for his two young sons and because God told him to do it.

Next, I googled up DARE, Drug Abuse Resistance Education. They started about the same time as Just Say No, and they were aimed at the same target market – youth. Their clubs operated out of schools all across the country, but unlike Just Say No, they are still going strong.

It wasn't necessary for me to google MADD, Mothers Against Drunk Driving. It has become probably the most recognized anti-alcohol organization in the world. Yes, I know, many would correct me and say they aren't necessarily against all alcohol consumption, but only when behind the wheel of a car. Tell that to a mother who's lost a loved one to a drunk driver.

There was one last thing on my scribbled dream notes – Carrolton, Kentucky. When I googled it, that horrible day of May 4, 1988 came rushing into my consciousness. A drunk driver had plowed into a school bus filled with kids returning from a field trip. Twenty-four youth were killed as well as three adults. Many more were injured.

` The original phone message had said to pay attention to my dreams. I *was* paying attention. I had just researched each item I had scribbled down on my paper, hadn't I? It was the *big question* that still eluded me – what was I supposed to do with this information? I got up and walked around the house a little. I went by the door that opened to the deck. I walked past it, but then I stopped, went back to the door and opened it. Oscar was still there, still messing with my running shoes. He looked up at me and barked a couple of times. Hey … what did that phone message this morning say about Oscar? It said he's a good dog, a smart dog too.

"Okay, I get it," I said to Oscar, "We are supposed to go running, but would you please tell me one thing? Who are those guys you're working with? You know, the Appalachian accent and the British accent, both on the other end of the seven sevens number." Oscar looked at me and slanted his head sideways, but he didn't say anything.

I got myself ready to go for a run. I went out on the deck to put my running shoes on, and Oscar and I took off down the road. We went a mile and then I jumped off the road and found another trail that would lead back to Perkin's Bluff. It wasn't the same route I had used three days ago with the Barkleys. Anyway, we didn't stay on it very long. I turned left onto a game trail I would follow through the woods every once in a while. In a quarter mile it passed old Albert Wilson's place. He was eighty-two when he died thirty years ago. He never married. There were a lot of stories about Albert. One of my favorites concerned a big old wild cherry tree that sat off about forty yards from the front porch of his little rickety frame house. It seemed that as Albert got older, he took a mind to get rid of the tree. He said, "It spoiled the view of the rise of that wooded area back behind it." He was discussing the situation with a friend of his one day, and his friend said it would take a while, but they could shoot it down. So that's what they did. Every time his friend would come by, the two of them would sit out on the porch with their 30-30 deer rifles and take several chunks out of that four-foot-wide cherry tree. Their target line was about three feet off the ground. Essentially what they were doing was working from the outside in. Sort of a 30-30 chain saw, but much slower. Eventually they whittled it down enough to where the weight in the top just knocked it down to the ground. I imagine they spent a lot of money on the bullets, but it was said that they got their money's worth out of it for the fun they had.

Oscar and I continued running, following the same game trail. It climbed up that "rise" behind where the shot-down cherry tree had been. Why Albert called it a rise, I'd never know. It was actually a pretty steep hill. Up on top, the trail leveled out and skirted a small cornfield used by hunters to draw deer into their kill zone. Two camouflaged tree shacks stood watch on the kill zone – one on each side, both of them up about thirty feet in a tree. It was an area I never ran in when deer season started up.

Then in another half mile we came to the place I had in mind. Up high on the hill we had a good view of what all the locals called "Dry Creek Holler". The valley down below was pierced by a dirt road which had an old-timey looking farm set back a ways, its pastures climbing the hills on the far side of the valley. Beautiful. Just beautiful. Oscar started rolling around in a grassy area. I said, why not and got down and rolled around with him.

When I got back up, my senses had been aroused, no, they had been ignited. I couldn't tell you exactly what happened, but in short order I would know, maybe not everything I wanted to know, but everything I needed to know. My thinking went something like this:

Terry Fox, a runner, but a runner with a major handicap – he only had one good leg.

Terry Fox, young man who truly wanted to help his fellow human beings.

Finn Weaver, a runner, but a runner with a major handicap – he is sixty-eight years old.

Finn Weaver, a man who truly wants to help his fellow human beings.

The world we live in is a world in big trouble. Of course, it always has been in big trouble. How did Solomon put it? "All is vanity; that which has been is what will be; there is nothing new under the sun; what is crooked cannot be made straight; to know wisdom, madness, and folly is grasping for the wind; to everything there is a season; for there is a time there for every purpose and for every work." Solomon said a lot more than that. The last thing I remember him saying in the book of Ecclesiastes was "Fear God and His commandments, For this is man's all. For God will bring every work into judgement, including every secret thing, whether good or evil."

I wasn't sure what to think or what to do. Those five items that flashed up on my mental screen were trying to tell me something. What was it?

The next thing that danced through my thought patterns was the first phone call late yesterday afternoon, "What if you could help millions of people, rather than a tiny handful?" I matched up that idea with what Terry Fox had actually done. Terry had gotten the attention of many millions of people who had donated money for cancer research. Is that what I was supposed to do? Mount a fundraiser for cancer research? No, I didn't think that was it. What then? Was it MADD, Mothers Against Drunk Driving? Was it Just Say No? That group didn't even exist anymore. Then it came to me. Didn't Solomon say, "Fear God and keep His commandments, For this is man's all." I felt like I was about to crack the code. I kept thinking about the incredible sacrifice Terry Fox made in order to help people. I picked up a stick and wrote in the dirt the word CANCER.

I thought about the Just Say No marathoner back in 1986. That runner was not Terry Fox. No, just an ordinary man. He was running to abolish use of illegal drugs. I wrote the word DRUGS in the dirt.

I thought MADD. They were trying to stamp out drunk drivers. I wrote ALCOHOL in the dirt.

I was still thinking things through and looking down at those three words. All three of these organizations had made valiant efforts at eliminating some loathsome, destructive affliction and deviltry that was designed to destroy mankind. Maybe some progress has been made. No doubt some breakthroughs have occurred in the battle with cancer. What about the other two – drugs and alcohol? I almost laughed. Anyone could see we are losing those battles.

So, I'm thinking, is it possible that although these three evils – cancer, drugs, alcohol are certainly worthy of the efforts, trials, and toils we've thrown at them; is it possible we've used the wrong approach all along? All of the research, advertising, rehab centers, wars on drugs, police interdiction, and the billions of dollars thrown at the problems have done very little to eliminate them.

What if we took a different approach? What if we go to God? Don't the scriptures tell us to place God first? And if we do that, all our needs will be met?

I was feeling it now. Things were coming together. I kept flashing back to the phone call – "Help millions of people". Then I remembered the dream, the message "The Boss" had left for me – "Terry Fox is waiting for you. He's wondering why you haven't started yet?" Then the heat in the soles of my feet and the fact that my running shoes, seemingly had a will and resolve bestowed on them from somewhere other than Earth.

It was coming, I could feel it – what I was supposed to do:

RUN

That was it, what I was supposed to do. But who for? What for? Was I supposed to run against drugs, drunk drivers, cancer?

No – Yes – Run for God first. Those things will be taken care of.

Run for God – This is man's all.

I'd really done it this time. I'd worked myself up into a frenzy, enough so that my new existence which was centered on Christian counselling had just taken a major detour. I was now going to be running for God. Did this mean I would not continue the counselling? I didn't know the answer to that, All I knew was I would be running for God because this is man's all.

CHAPTER 8

The next day I made preparations to start my RFG-TIMA, Running For God – This Is Man's All. First, I went into Clarksville and found a good outfitting shop where I purchased a runner's backpack – not too big, and it rode on my back and shoulders comfortably. I figured I could carry about twenty pounds of food, thermo running gear, and an emergency shelter without sacrificing very much efficiency in my running stride.

Next, I found a sporting goods store that specialized in stenciling and printing logos and signs on clothing and gear. I had them imprint all my stuff with RFG-TIMA. I figured the acronym would be helpful in explaining the motivation which seemed to be propelling me into this unexpected phase of my new existence. You see, I had no idea of exactly what I was supposed to do, other than run. I certainly was not going to be mounting some big publicity program to draw attention to RFG-TIMA. On the other hand, how was I going to help "millions of people" if no one knew what I was running for. Like a bell had rung in my head, the answer showed up immediately: I was running for God. If he was going to convert my efforts into helping "millions", that was His business. My job was to run for Him, and already, the idea of doing that, of keeping it simple, was starting to feel pretty good.

When I got back home from Clarksville, I checked my phone for anything that had a 423-777-7777 return number. There was nothing on it. But I made two calls of my own: one to Renae Holsclaw and the other to my son Aaron in Knoxville. When Renae picked up, I heard her say, "Talk to Coach Finn, Wendy. Come on, talk to him." I heard a baby mumbling and chattering like a little bird.

"Hey, that's pretty good," I said.

"She loves to talk to people." You could hear the pride in momma's voice.

"Her name is Wendy?"

"Yeah, Wendy April Holsclaw."

"Beautiful name. I like it. I called to let you know I'll be out of town for a week or so, but I'll be back before your hearing. Just wanted to see if there's anything you need me for before I go."

"I guess not. I'm getting worried though – what the judge might do."

"That's to be expected. But I'm praying for you, and I hope you've been going to the Lord and opening your heart to Him."

"I'm sorry, I haven't been doing much of that."

"Why not? I'm certain His will won't be done unless you're praying for it."

"Maybe that's what I'm afraid of." Her words would turn out to be prophetic.

I called Aaron and he was quite interested in hearing any news on my counselling. I told him only generalities about my two most active cases. Names and details I left out. I figured that was something my clients were entitled to – confidentiality. I told him I was hitting the road tomorrow morning on the first leg of my RFG-TIMA.

"You're what?"

"I'm putting Oscar and Shirley in a kennel tonight. Tomorrow morning at seven o'clock I'm shutting the house down and I'll be starting to run the 224 miles to your house. I plan on it taking about 12 days running at an 18-mile-a-day pace."

He was laughing like a drunk monkey.

"What's so funny?"

"You, Dad. That's the goofiest thing I've heard in a long time. Even if you were crazy enough to try it, what does it have to do with your counselling?"

"Nothing, maybe. I'm not sure. It's something I have to do."

"Something you have to do? I don't get it."

"I wasn't sure you would. I'm not even sure I get it. I'm doing it for God; that's all I'm sure about. You can understand that, can't you?"

"Uh, if anybody else said that, I'd probably be calling the psycho ward. With you saying it, I guess all I can say is good luck and how can I help you?"

"Well, actually, that's why I've chosen your house to run to. I have to be back in Clarksville the very next day. I was hoping you'd drive me back home."

"Yeah, I guess I could do that. I mean, you know, as long as I don't miss a workday."

"No problem. That will be on a Sunday. I need to be with my client on Monday morning. That's when she goes to court."

"Okay, Dad. I'll commit to being your return driver. What else can I do?"

"Just don't commit me to the psycho ward."

Things were rushing along wildly; careening was maybe a better word. Maybe I should have been getting worried about this rapid progression of events – this new existence of mine. But now I was way too busy to fret over such meager concerns. I needed to get Oscar and Shirley to a kennel and then prepare for my first day on the road, running for God. I changed my mind about the kennel. Instead, I called Buff, my closest and most trusted neighbor. He said yes to my request that he come by and feed and water Oscar and Shirley, and in general, keep an eye on things. "Buff" was short for "Buffalo", the nickname he played with as a defensive tackle at Vanderbilt.

I began stuffing the backpack with food, running gear, and the emergency first responder blanket I had purchased. I had only an amateur's knowledge of how to prepare for 12 days of heavy running. My hopes were that I wouldn't really need most of the stuff I was packing. I intended to eat out of convenience stores or fast-food restaurants, and I planned on diving into motels when the sun went down. What could possibly go wrong? What could possibly prevent me from doing God's will – running for Him?

That night when I went to bed it was like I'd gone backwards in time, back to my playing days and the first couple of years coaching 8th grade basketball. Back in the early days I was just an average basketball player, both in the Navy and then in junior college. I never played on any high school teams, just pick-up games around St. Louis where I grew up. I could never sleep on nights before games, playing or coaching. Not then or much later at Austin Peay. I was too keyed up. And that's the way it was on the night before I would launch the second phase of my new existence – RFG-TIMA

CHAPTER 9

It was a relief to get out of bed and put on a pot of coffee. At least the frustration of no sleep had ended. I was in the den when I went to my knees in prayer. "Dear Heavenly Father, I thank you for this day, this beautiful day You've given that I may do my best to serve You. I'm not sure what You've got in store for me, Father, but I pray You'll give me the strength, the faith, and the love in my heart to do Your will. I ask You to be with Renae and Wendy, and to be with Justin and Julie. Protect them from evil, Lord, bring them along the path to open their hearts to Jesus. Father, be with all of those in this hurting world that need You so much. May every heart, every soul, open the door and ask Jesus to take them. In Jesus name I pray. Amen."

I let Oscar out of the house so he could take care of his early morning business and then I dressed for an 18-mile run. I ate a huge bowl of oatmeal and topped that off with three bananas. I went out to fetch Oscar, but he wouldn't come back in the house. I knew why. He knew something was up. He wouldn't come in until I ran a mile with him through the woods. The way I figured it, I only had seventeen more miles to do that first day.

Here we go. Running for God by a 68-year-old ex-basketball coach may have looked and sounded strange to probably anybody. Not to me. It felt like the most natural thing in the world. I was wearing a long-sleeved T-shirt with material designed to wick away moisture and a light running jacket over it. It was a chilly morning, right at 40 degrees, but still I only wore running shorts, not sweatpants. On my head I had a tan, broad rimmed bush hat, and I wore light running gloves. I drank a lot of water and then slipped on the backpack. I said to Oscar, "Be a good boy. I'll see you in twelve days." I gave him a big hug and noticed Shirley looking at me strangely. I picked her up and rubbed the back of her neck and said, "Be a good kitty." I locked the door behind me and started running for God.

It was only four miles to highway 48, the first of many on which I would have to be extremely cautious while running – deliberate. This section of 48 was two- lane. The shoulders were wide enough to avoid being pancaked by the 60-mph traffic, but just barely in a lot of places. When the back road I was on came out at 48, I went into a tiny country store on the near side of the highway.

"Coach Finn, you're not running to Nashville, are you? (Nashville was 50 miles away.) I didn't hear your truck."

"No, Marie, I'm running to Knoxville." I went to the drink cooler, picked out a Gatorade and placed it by the check out.

"Well, I reckon since you're running all the way to Knoxville, let me buy that drink for you."

"Thanks Marie, and God bless you." I saw her pick up her phone as I was walking out the door.

It was 10:00 AM, I had five miles under my belt, only twelve more to go. I started running again staying on the left side of the roadway, facing oncoming northbound traffic. I was running probably in the neighborhood of 12-minute-miles, awfully slow for younger runners, not so bad for 68-year-olds. Other than paying close attention to cars and trucks whizzing by me only six or seven feet away, my mind was a carefree summer breeze. I was at peace, I was free, and I was running for God. I was wondering if today I would experience the silky-smooth euphoria called "the runner's high"? Back in the days that my runs would sometimes take me as far as eight or ten miles, the intoxicating rush of endorphins slashing through my brain was always more than welcome. Scientist call endorphins the body's "happy chemicals". They are released when you experience prolonged stress and then the nicest thing happens: pain and discomfort is reduced and replaced with a sense of joy and wellbeing. Whoopie! I knew without a doubt that in a couple more hours I would probably need some reduced pain and discomfort. The joy and wellbeing wouldn't be bad either.

The day was warming up. I removed the lightweight jacket and stuffed it in my backpack. I slurped down the last of the Gatorade and pressed on – the 12-minute running miles were now increased to 13-minute jogs. The beautiful Tennessee fall-foliage made good company for me. I was already feeling a bit of the isolation that solo long-distance runners must feel. Well, at least the ones I'd read about. They said isolation and loneliness was all part of the game – part of the mystique – part of the DNA of humans who use their feet to trod thousands of miles. Was I going to run thousands of miles? Who knew? I didn't. But I did know that a Montgomery County Sheriff's deputy had his cruiser pulled over on the shoulder fifty yards in front of me.

As I approached, I could see that the officer was outside the cruiser, waiting for me. I recognized him immediately – Danny Tankersley. "Hey Danny, what brings you out to this end of the county?"

"You, coach Finn."

"Me?"

"Yeah. You know Marie, back at the store. She called in and told dispatch that you were running to Knoxville."

"I am."

He looked perplexed, wrinkled his brow and scratched at his ear. "I guess there's nothing illegal about that, but I guess I ought to ask you. Are you okay? Do you feel all right?"

"I feel fine."

"Coach, do you mind if I ask you another question?"

"That's fine."

"Why are you running to Knoxville?"

The sweat was dripping off my nose. The sun was really stirring things up now. I wished I had greased myself up with sun- block. Danny was waiting for an answer. I said, "See this?" I showed him the stencil on my backpack RFG-TIMA. "That's what I'm doing. Running for God-This Is Man's All."

"Sure, sure, I see. That sounds great. But you know, it's pretty dangerous out here on an open road like this."

"Danny, don't worry. I'll be fine."

"How far you going today?"

"I'd like to get another ten miles, just past Cumberland Furnace."

"That's across the county line. You'll be in Dickson County. Somebody going to pick you up?"

"Not that I know of."

"Well, uh, where you going to sleep?"

"A motel if I can find one."

"There's no motels anywhere around there."

He was right. I knew it before he asked me. To be honest, I was looking forward to sleeping out in the woods. It had been a long time since I had "roughed it" and I guess I wanted to see if I could still hack it.

Danny moved on. He said he didn't think it was safe, me being out here, but he didn't reckon he could do anything about it. I told him not to worry and "God bless you, Danny", and continued running southbound.

This section of highway 48 began heaving up and down as if it were a throw rug being shaken by hand by an energetic house maid. Some of the hills were easily eight percent grades. I had driven this road hundreds of times but had never given heed to what torture it might be like to run its punishing hills. I was paying attention now. Each summit became harder and harder to achieve. My pace would have put me in last place in a turtle marathon. But I kept running … uh, I kept slogging upwards until each new crest had been conquered.

Eventually I came to a half-mile of flat roadway. I could see a country store down near the end, before yet another incline waiting for me. I decided to lunch at the store. It was 2:00 in the afternoon and I figured Cumberland Furnace was only another two miles. The man behind the counter paid no attention to me as I walked over to the warmer where left over breakfast biscuits were half price this time of day. I grabbed a couple of ham and egg biscuits and then picked up a couple of granola bars off the rack. I went to the cooler and found me a 24-ounce Gatorade, paid for my stuff and headed back outside. A small table with three chairs was down at the end of the walkway. I unhooked the backpack, took it off, and sat down. That was my first mistake of the day. In thirty minutes it was going to take a Herculean effort for me to get back on my feet and slog out the last three miles of the day.

When I finally got to my feet it was close to 3 o'clock. I limped back inside the store and went back to the drink cooler and picked out two more 24-ounce Gatorades. I spotted a fruit stand and grabbed all the apples, oranges, and bananas I could hold and deposited my bounty down in front of the check out. The same man behind the counter rang up the bill.

"Thirteen forty-nine," he said.

I gave him my debit card, he ran it through, and I said, "Thank you."

"Would you like a bag?"

"Sure," I said. "Thank you."

He was a very dark-skinned man, very black hair, and dark eyes. "You must be walking a long way. You have no car."

"I'm running to Knoxville. I'm running for God."

"Running for God. A Buddhist might say you are seeking enlightenment."

"Are you a Buddhist?"

"No. Many in my family are Buddhist."

"Muslim?"

"No."

"Hindu?"

"No."

"Are you an atheist?"

"No, I'm a student of many spiritual persuasions."

"Okay, I think I got you. You must be an agnostic. You don't disbelieve in God, but you must have infallible evidence that God actually exist."

"Most would say that is the case. I am currently a member of the Unitarian Universalist. I attend a church in Nashville."

"The Unitarians, I believe two of their earliest constituents were Henry David Thoreau and Thomas Jefferson."

He offered an inquisitive smile. "You are Unitarian?"

"No, I'm Methodist."

"Methodist, very interesting. I have visited several mainline evangelical churches – the Baptist, the Church of Christ, and the Pentecostals. But I've not had the pleasure to be a guest of the Methodist."

I felt like this man was a true theologian. Was he a Christian? I didn't know. "My little church is not far from here. You should come and worship with us soon."

"Yes, I think that I would learn much from such a visit. So, tell me about this "running for God" you mentioned."

I gave him the quick explanation of what I was doing. He didn't seem surprised at all. Maybe he understood it better than I did. We talked for a few more minutes and I gave him directions to the church I attend.

I stuffed the fruit and Gatorades into the backpack, put it back on my sore shoulders and headed off down the road. As I approached the tiny hamlet of Cumberland Furnace, I began to notice that some very nasty blisters on my feet and toes were demanding attention. Thank goodness I had packed a few first aid items. I would use them to treat the blisters when I stopped for the night. But there was something else distressing me that had nothing to do with the physical abuse I was imposing on my body. I turned around and started back towards the little country store. My pace picked up. I had a new pep in my step. The various pains which had built up in the seventeen miles of running, they subsided a little bit, they backed off just a tad.

Twenty minutes later I stumbled back into the store, out of breath, soaked all the way through from my sweat, and I'm sure with a look of utter desperation on my face. The dark-skinned man was still there, working on a display rack on my side of the check-out-counter. He looked smaller than he had before.

He looked up at me, surprised, and said, "Are you all right?"

"Yes. I came back to tell you that Jesus Christ is the Way, the Truth, and the Life. Believe me, I understand that Unitarians are good people. They are serious about studying all aspects of all theologies. I have Unitarians in my family. They have been the best people I've ever known. They work hard, they love people, all people. I understand all of that. But I got to thinking, just a little while ago, when I left here. What if I kept on running and never told you that Jesus is the only way to the Father, you know, the one Father all religions seek. Then I realized, that's why I'm out here running under my banner of RFG-TIMA. I'm out here to proclaim Jesus Christ to this world suffering in sin. It looks like I've become the shouting nut case on the street corner waving the Bible and warning that Armageddon is at hand."

There it was. I got it out – most of it. Oh, there was plenty more, but I was about out of gas. I said, "God bless you. I hope to see you at church." I headed out the door and started back up that hill a second time.

CHAPTER 10

I'm not saying my first night in the woods was fun, but it could have been a lot worse. As things turned out, it would be the only night that I had to sleep outdoors in the elements. It started after I had passed through the tiny burg of Cumberland Furnace, whose history in the early 1800's had seen it being an iron works town. Cannon balls from its furnace were used by Andrew Jackson at New Orleans in the War of 1812. The current population of Cumberland Furnace was 693 souls. There are plenty of woodlands in the area and after I had cleared through the village, I walked into the woods far enough to be away from any traffic, or houses, or people. The first thing I did was go to work on the blisters which if not treated would surely put an end to any running when the new day started. First, I popped the blisters with a pin and forced the fluid out. I dabbed them with a little hydrogen peroxide and then a little antibiotic cream and then a little moleskin to cover the whole shebang. I knew that redoing that exact treatment twice a day would eventually turn the painful blisters into tough, leathery dermis and future 17 to 20 mile running days would have one less problem to deal with.

Next, I put together a little shelter. I gathered downed limbs and branches and stacked them against a cross piece limb that I hung between two small trees. I piled on anything else close by and put together a bed of leaves for a sleeping mat. My home for the night wouldn't help much if hard rain were to cascade down from the skies, but it was only for one night and I guess, truth be told, it *was* fun building it – all a part of roughing it.

The only thing left to do was to eat and pray. I did plenty of both. I guess it was close to eight o'clock; the sun had departed over an hour ago. I put on dry sweats and unwrapped the survival blanket, crawled inside it and laid down on my pallet of fall leaves. Couldn't sleep for a while. Just zeroed out and listened to the sounds of the night.

When I got up the next morning, I felt like I'd been run over by a freight train, and what was left of me had been stampeded by a herd of elephants. I wasn't sure I could walk or even bend down enough to put my shoes on. Eventually I got myself out of the woods and started walking towards the town of Charlotte, Tennessee, the Dickson County Seat. It would take a half hour before my battered body would be able to run. While I walked, I munched the last of the fruit and granola bars. Washed it down with the last of the Gatorade. I was dying for a cup of coffee. It would have to wait. Charlotte was four miles away.

I started running again and I was getting close to Charlotte. A Dickson County Sheriff's Department cruiser pulled over in front of me, just like Danny Tankersley had done yesterday. I didn't know this new deputy, but he was outside the cruiser waiting for me. "Are you Coach Finnegan Weaver?" The officer had Sergeant stripes, no small thing in a county sheriff's department pecking order. He looked like he'd been around, like he knew what he was doing.

"Yes sir. That would be me." I pulled the straps from my shoulders and dropped the backpack to the ground. Sweat was dripping from my upper lip.

"Deputy Tankersley, up in Montgomery County, called me last night and said you were coming this way. I wanted to come out here and see if you needed anything. I think what you are doing is a great thing."

"Thank you, sergeant. I didn't get your name."

"Mincey. Sergeant Gerald Mincey. It sure is good to meet you."

"Indeed, same here. Gerald, tell me. Do you know where a man might get a cup of coffee around here?" He picked up my backpack and put it in the cruiser and ushered me in behind it. A mile down the road we pulled into a little homey diner. You could smell the sausage and country ham when we walked in, but what I smelled mostly was the coffee. There were a few customers scattered around, most of them at a big communal table. We took a booth off to the side.

A waitress was coming our way. Sergeant Mincey said, "Darlene, would you please bring us fresh coffee?"

"You got it, Sergeant. Y'all gonna' have somethin' ta eat?"

"I don't know." Mincey was looking at me.

"Darlene," I said. "I'd like to try your country ham, three scrambled eggs, grits and biscuits."

"Comin' up." I guess she knew the sergeant was only having coffee.

"Coach," Mincey settled back and I thought I saw him flick off the scanner attached to his gun belt, "Some of your teams were legends around here. I remember that year you knocked off Western Kentucky to earn a spot in the NCAA tournament."

"Oh yeah. That was a special bunch of players. Great memories."

"You retired, what was it? Six years ago?"

"Yes, that'd be about right."

"Last night when Tankersley called and said you were running to Knoxville for God … um … at first, I thought he was putting me on. I said, 'Coach Weaver must be in his late sixties. How's he gonna' do it?' But you know what? I didn't question the "God part". Not one bit. I've seen men do it before. When a man puts God first in his life, he can do most anything."

"Thanks for the confidence. I hope I can make it to Knoxville. This morning about sun-up I wasn't sure."

"Where'd you sleep last night, Coach?"

"I slept in the woods, just this side of Cumberland Furnace. I think I'll be in a motel tonight."

"How far you going today?"

"I'd like to make it to Kingston Springs. That's about fifteen miles, isn't it?"

"Yes sir, it is. I know they've got two motels." He stopped, seemed to be thinking about something, and started again, "Coach, I'm wondering if you'd be interested in talking to some of our prisoners over at the jail?"

"Sure. What do you have in mind?"

"We have a jail chaplaincy program and we do the best we can, you know. We have Bible study classes, AA and NA programs, GED classes, and other things we try to do. Whenever we can get a guest speaker, we like to bring them in and give a motivational talk. We could bring you in this evening, if you'd be interested."

"I'd like to do it Sergeant. But somebody will have to come and get me. Hopefully I'll be at my motel fifteen miles away by tonight."

"No problem, Coach. I'm the jail chaplain. I'll pick you up and return you to the motel. How does 7 o'clock sound?"

"Sounds good, Sergeant." I was starting on my second cup of coffee and eyeing the country ham platter that Darlene was setting down in front of me.

The running that second day just about did me in. When I got to the motel, I borrowed a bathroom scale from the manager and checked my weight. I had lost eleven pounds the first two days – from 250 down to 239. On my six-foot, five-inch frame most of the loss was up around my neck, arms, face, and shoulders. The belly-fat is always the last to go. Sergeant Mincey knocked on my door at 6:30 and we drove all the way back to Charlotte where the county jail was.

The jail was larger than I had imagined. Sergeant Mincey said that the inmate population averaged around 250 men and 50 women. Not all of the inmates were serving less than one-year sentences. He said about twenty-five percent were actually state prisoners who were transferred to certain county jails on account of overflows in the state prisons. When we entered the jail, we worked our way back through four or five security doors, and eventually arrived at the chapel. Mincey looked at me and said, "You sure you're good with this, Coach?" I nodded my approval. Mincey pushed an intercom button on the wall and spoke into it, "Bring the prisoners on down, Corporal Barnes. We're in the chapel waiting."

A couple of minutes later about thirty prisoners were ushered into the chapel by six or seven armed correctional officers who took positions at the back of the room. The prisoners were clad in dingy orange jump suits. There were no women. The men all got settled down in the first five rows of beat-up church pews. Sergeant Mincey and I were up front. He stood behind a pulpit. I was off to his side.

There was a light hum of chatter and clouded expectation crawling through the chapel. Mincey started things off. "Gentlemen, we've got a special treat for you tonight. I'm just going to get out of his way. Please welcome Coach Finnegan Weaver, retired Austin Peay University head basketball coach."

I looked out at the prisoners, many adorned with prison tattoos. Some I recognized as gang ID's, some satanic, and some were religious in nature – crosses, portraits of Mary, etc. The one that got my attention the most was on a prisoner's knuckles – five letters – J E S U S. I had not spent any time planning or preparing what I might say to these men. I guess I figured what would come out of my mouth was going to come out, whether I planned it, or not.

"Guys, I'd start with a good prison joke, but I've never heard a good prison joke. Looking around at this place, I can see why. I don't know why you are here. I've heard that some folks who find themselves incarcerated say they know why they are locked up, and that they understand that they should be locked up. They believe prison is the best place for them – the place they are supposed to be. I have no way of knowing if they are right. Maybe some of you feel the same way. My guess is it wouldn't be very many of you. But I heard a story one time that I think may explain part of the reasons men and women find themselves in terrible situations. Actually, it's not just a story.

Its's about a young man I met one day when I was down in Memphis on a recruiting trip. Most of the day I spent talking to several families about their son playing basketball at Austin Peay. Well, my work was done, it was getting late in the day and so I started the four-hour drive back to Clarksville. I guess I was twenty miles out of Memphis, heading back this way. There was nobody with me. I'd made this recruiting trip a solo trip. Sometimes I felt I'd do better with no other coaches with me. So, anyway, I pulled into a truck stop to get some coffee for the long drive back home. I got my coffee, but before I left, I drifted over to a display island that had mostly religious and inspirational books on it. I was looking at a certain book that I was interested in and realized there was a young man leafing through another copy of the same book. We struck up a conversation and it didn't take long for me to realize that this young man was a very unique, a very special individual.

"He said he'd been travelling from Oklahoma City for two days. He didn't have a car. He was hitch-hiking. He explained to me that he was a missionary on his way to Pakistan. His home church back in Oklahoma City had provided him with an airline ticket from New York to Pakistan, but in order to save money, he was travelling across the U.S. in the least expensive way possible – hitch-hiking. I offered the young man a ride to Nashville. He said there was another church there that had agreed to help out by providing him a home to stay in for the overnight. Mark, that was his name, he left the truck stop with me and we started the drive towards Nashville. We also started a conversation that would last well into the late hours of the night. Mostly, I was asking Mark about his background, his interest, his motivation to being a Christian missionary.

"As we got close to Nashville, Mark phoned his friends there from the church, but they couldn't be reached, no connection was made. I invited Mark to spend the night at my home and the next morning I'd drive him down to Nashville. Mark said that sounded good.

"When we got to my home up near Clarksville, my wife wasn't all that surprised I'd brought a stranger home to spend the night with us. Like me, she was totally taken in by Mark's positive attitude, the joy for life he exuded, and his determination to get on the other side of the world in order to embark on his work as a Christian Missionary."

I looked out at the prisoners and I could sense that they were beginning to wonder where this story was going. Were they wasting their time, coming to the chapel to listen to some old dried-up basketball coach rattle off stale and threadbare accounts of his highway adventures?

"Fellas, here's why I'm telling you about the young missionary named Mark. I think there's something in his story that resonates with all of us, especially when we find ourselves in serious trouble. You see, as my wife and I sat there talking with Mark, we learned that like everybody else, Mark wasn't perfect. He'd made serious mistakes in his past. He told us he'd been raised in a solid Christian family, and that as a young teenage boy he accepted Jesus Christ as his Savior. He went to church with the rest of his family, and everyone that knew him felt like Mark was on the right path – that in his heart there existed a strong bond with God. But, as the case is so often, Satan found a way to interfere; found a way to shatter Mark's trust in God. At age nineteen, Mark fell in with a group of knot-heads who thought that partying and binge drinking started every afternoon at five o'clock and didn't end until much later, after damage had been done.

"He was arrested one night for DUI after having crossed over the double line and crashing into an on-coming vehicle. Inside that vehicle was a family of four, all transported to the hospital with serious injuries. Mark was transported to the local jail and because of the serious nature of the charges, an extremely high bail was set. His family didn't even attempt to make bail. Mark's father was probably thinking this was the time for tough love.

"There he was – nineteen, his first time in jail. Nobody was coming to save him. He'd heard plenty of stories about what could happen to newcomers inside the dark, dangerous walls of jails and prisons. He couldn't believe this was happening to him. He couldn't believe God was abandoning him. That first night they had kept him in an isolated cell – nobody in there with him, just Mark. But the guards had told him that unless he made bail, tomorrow morning he was going to general population. He couldn't sleep that night. He sat on the edge of his bunk, his mind working against him, telling him he was doomed, telling him that undoubtedly God was punishing him, deserting him to a fate too hideous to believe. He just couldn't believe God would do this to him. 'Haven't I loved You?' Mark asked. 'Haven't I accepted Jesus? Haven't I tried to do right?' All night Mark questioned God as to why He had deserted him. The more he thought about it the more lost and alone he became. 'Why?' he demanded. Weeping, distraught, empty, abandoned, and guilty, Mark asked one last time, 'Why did You let this happen to me?'

"God finally responded. 'Mark, my love for you has never ceased. What did I say to you last night before you got behind the wheel of your car? I said, don't do this. Remember? I didn't drop you, Mark. You dropped me. And when you began weaving all over the road, I could have let you run off into the trees, or down by that low stretch, into the river. I thought maybe you'd see I was protecting you. Finally, when you hit the other car, Mark, why do you think you weren't injured? Why do you think you survived? And what about the family, Mark? What if you had killed the two children? What if you had killed all four of them? Do you think you'd ever get out of prison?'"

I stopped talking. The chapel was very quiet. I could see that some of the prisoners had dropped their heads a little, their hands cupped to hold them. Other prisoners did the opposite; they laughed and acted detached and unconcerned.

"You know, men, I never asked Mark if he actually heard God's voice, or rather, it was just something that he felt. What difference would it have made? God spoke to him. As things turned out, Mark did a prison sentence and when he got out, he became a pastor. He got into more trouble, but eventually he dedicated his life to missionary work.

"Thank you for having me here." I looked at Sergeant Mincey, "Thank you Chaplain for asking me. May God bless each and every one of you. If you ever need me for anything, I'm not hard to find, just up the road in Montgomery County."

I turned to walk away but a prisoner shouted out loudly, "Coach Finnegan, how do you know this guy, Mark, stayed dry? I mean, you know, how do you know he didn't fall off the alcohol wagon, that he didn't become a drunk again?"

"Because he told me."

"Uh, just because he said he stayed sober, you believed him?"

"Yes, I believed him."

"Why? Or maybe the question should be *how*? I mean, you know, here's a guy locked up for a serious DUI, and he gets into more trouble later on. How could you believe a guy like that?" There was a low scattering of jabber moving amongst all of the prisoners.

"The reason I believed him is because something similar happened to me when I was a young man. I was struggling with drugs and alcohol myself. One night I said four words and my whole life changed. The night I talked to Mark, he told me that when he continued to get into trouble, there was one night when it all came to a head. He was on his knees, literally in the gutter, and somehow he found himself saying the same four words I had said."

The prisoner really wanted to know about those four words. I could tell he was serious when he asked me, "What were the four words?"

"Jesus, please take me," I said.

CHAPTER 11

The next morning, I checked my weight again. I was down another four pounds. I reworked the blisters and then I checked all my equipment. There was no sense hanging around Kingston Springs, so I wolfed down the continental breakfast in the motel lobby – lots of bananas and granola. I must have drunk five cups of coffee. Running out of Kingston Springs, I had to veer north about three miles in order to pick up highway 70. When I hit it, I turned right and headed for Nashville. I settled into what I thought was a pretty good pace. I'm sure to anyone else it looked like the "slow boat to China" you used to hear about. You don't hear much about it anymore. Come to think of it, most of the aphorisms and one-liners I use are not heard anymore. Hey, getting old is hard enough, it's not fair they even take your language away. I remember an old bluegrass album entitled *Old And In The Way*. It has a cold bite to it, like you're not needed anymore. Maybe that's what this "Running For God – This Is Mans's All" is all about – my striving to not be irrelevant, to not be discarded. No, that wasn't it. Deep down I knew this "new existence" I set out on ten days ago was important. I felt like it was what my whole life had come to. It was to be the defining crucible of my life. Any prior achievements or accomplishments meant nothing. *This* was it. This new existence, this Running For God – This Is Man's All, this was it. This was everything. When I looked at it that way, I quickly forgot about being sixty-eight years old. I felt more like thirty-five. Funny, isn't it? When God has you by the ears, you feel younger, not older. I picked up my pace a little more. Downtown Nashville was still twenty miles away.

It was a good day for running. The late fall temperature was sixty-two degrees. I passed through the tiny burg of Pegram, a railroad stop from the nineteenth century. Now days it was home to some of the original families of that period and to many newcomers to middle Tennessee. The old families still fished the Harpeth River, still scoured the woods for ginseng and a few were still distilling moonshine liquor. The more recent arrivals were interested in living close to Nashville, but not living in it. Many of them were connected to Nashville's thriving music, entertainment, and tourist industries. Highway 70 runs alongside the Harpeth River for a couple of miles. It meanders up on the side of some hills which didn't leave much of a shoulder to run on. On-coming traffic came very close to knocking me back against the rock walls of those hills. I kept thinking surely I could have chosen a safer road to run on. In about five more miles I passed the 70-south cut-off that went through the sprawling Nashville suburb of Bellevue. Dozens of square miles of crammed subdivisions and commercial development. I stayed on the main 70 corridor and by four o'clock I was coming into Nashville proper. I dived into the first of many motels on this western side of the city. I knew I was still eight miles from downtown Nashville, but I wasn't running another step. After checking in, I found my room and dropped onto the bed and didn't move for an hour and a half. When I finally got up, I noticed for the first time in the last three days that my cell phone was dead, no charge. I found the charger in a side pocket of my backpack and plugged it in. While it was charging, I showered and dressed. I checked the phone. No problem; it had plenty of juice. I stuck it in my pocket as I left the motel room.

I had noticed a restaurant across the street from the motel. It looked like a large family eatery, you know, one of the well-known chains that served up monumental proportions of all-American chicken and beef, potatoes, salads, casseroles, pot pies, and fat, gooey deserts. I couldn't wait to get seated and dig in. I gave the menu back to the waitress and headed for the buffet. When she checked on me a few minutes later, she said, "I should have brought you a wheelbarrow."

"Don't worry," I said, "I'll pay double." She was laughing as she walked away.

Then, after having decimated most of the buffet dishes, I summoned my waitress over to my table. I smiled up at her and said, "I noticed you serve strawberry pie by the slice."

She looked at me with a decidedly troubled gaze in her eyes, "Yes sir, that's right." She was looking more worried each second.

"So, you think, just possibly, you might be able to serve me a whole strawberry pie?"

The worried look vanished from her face, "Oh sure. We sell whole pies to go home with folks all the time. You might want to look at the menu again. We have five or six selections."

"Thank you, but I'll just have the strawberry pie, uh, you know, the whole pie. But I won't be taking it home with me. And … oh, could you bring me more coffee, please?"

As I enjoyed my strawberry pie and coffee, I finally got around to checking any phone messages I might have missed. There was a call from my son Aaron, a call from Buffalo, my neighbor, and several junk calls. Aaron and Buffalo had left voice messages. I was about to cue them up, but I saw one more voice message from 423-777-7777. I listened to it first: "Witnessing for Jesus at the jail. Excellent, keep up the good work." That was it. That was the entire message.

I felt like laughing, but I couldn't. There wasn't anything funny about it. Evidently someone, or *something* was keeping a close watch on my activities. Was it God? I was thinking *who else could it be?* By now these strange events were becoming so routine, I was close to just accepting them as no big deal. No big deal? Really? I didn't think so. Then, the notion flew through my head – *no it wasn't God*, that is if you believed God didn't have an Appalachian accent. Whoever left the message definitely *had* an Appalachian accent. It was the same voice from the message stating that *the word's getting around. Your counselling is getting off to a good start. But what if you could help millions of people rather than a tiny handful? Think about it and pay attention to your dreams.* There was no doubt about it. It was the same voice. Then I remembered that later that night, in my dream, there was that clipped, chiseled English voice that answered my phone call with *Before Time – Beyond Creation, may I help you?* And I remembered that voice saying, *you can call us back anytime you have a question.* Are you kidding me? The first voice was a real-life Appalachian accent. No big mystery. I was awake and listening to the person's message. The fact that he had insider's information about my new existence, well, now … that certainly did have a handful of mystery. The second voice, The English patrician, that voice was inside a dream. The weird thing, the elephant in the room … both voices came from the same phone number. Okay, so what? People do that all the time – take something from the real world and conveniently insert it into their dream world. I must have done that, what was it, four or five nights ago? I must have inserted the phone number into my dream. Then I remembered, again, *you can call us back anytime you have a question.* I started dialing 423-777-7777.

"Beyond Time – Before Creation, may I help you?" It was the crisp, perfectly enunciated English voice.

"Yes, you certainly can help me. The last time I talked with you, I believe you said I could call you back if I had any questions. Well … I've got plenty of questions."

"Lovely. Let me see if I can transfer you to the appropriate party." There was some crinkly static on the line and what sounded like a solar wind whipping through colliding galaxies.

"Hello."

"Yes, I'd like to speak to the big boss." I realized how num-skulled my request must have sounded. I tried again, "I mean God. I'm sorry, I know you must think I'm crazy. It's just, who else could this phone number belong to if it isn't God?"

"This phone number, you say? What's so unusual about my phone number?"

"Your number is 423-777-7777 isn't it?"

"No, my number is 423-562-0419."

Okay, I thought I was starting to see the picture – another brain tease. Or, maybe this time, a brain freeze. Then it hit me. The voice I was talking to was the Appalachian voice. I was sure it was the same man. "So, did your receptionist, you know, the English guy, did he just transfer my call to you, or not?"

"What receptionist? My phone was ringing and I picked up your call."

My annoyance, not to mention my confusion, was starting to escalate. "Now, look mister, I know you called me five nights ago saying my counselling was off to a good start and helping millions of people and to pay attention to my dreams. Do you deny making that call?" He didn't say anything. I waited. He still didn't say anything. "Well?" I said. He didn't say anything. "Not only that, you called today and said, 'Good job on witnessing for Jesus at the jail.' Whoever you are and whatever you're doing, I think you owe me some kind of explanation."

"I reckon you gotta' good point there. Where do you want me to start?"

"At the beginning."

"Do you mean THE BEGINNING, or do you mean when I first became aware of your new existence?"

Very funny, I was thinking, but what I said was, "Why don't we just do the new existence thing for now. Keep it simple."

My waitress drifted towards me and placed my check on the table, "We're closing in ten minutes," she said.

I put the phone down and grabbed some cash out of my billfold. When I picked the phone up, the line was dead. The reception bars were gone, my conversation with mystery Appalachian Man was gone. I cued up the 423-777-7777 call and tried it again.

"Beyond time – Before Creation, may I help you?" It was the English man.

"Yes, I just lost my connection with the Appalachian man. Could you get him back for me?"

"Please hold." I heard the same solar wind and thunderous upheavals from somewhere that I didn't think could have been from this Earth. Then I heard a busy signal like any normal phone would give.

The English voice was back, "Coach Finn, I'm sorry, that line is busy at the moment. Is there a message you'd like me to convey?"

You talk about a brain freeze … I'm thinking, now, how about a *brain squeeze*? "I just talked with the guy a minute ago. He said his number was 423-562- … uh, I can't remember the rest of it. Do you have it?" The line went dead again. That was it for the night. I figured I'd better get back to the motel for some much needed rest. Tomorrow's eighteen miles through the middle of downtown Nashville would not be easy.

CHAPTER 12

The new day started off with another cold morning. I wore sweats, not running shorts. It was 10:30 in the morning when I sat down on a park bench in a little city park, just off Charlotte Avenue. Downtown was very close now, about four miles east. I was drinking water from my plastic water jug when I saw the old man coming my way. He was wearing a large, insulated, beaten up winter jacket over a ragged hoody. His almost white beard bounced out a couple of inches from his pale black skin. His eyes drooped under heavy lids but had a surprising hint of sparkle in them. Worn out denim pants and tattered work boots tried hard to protect his lower half from the cold morning. He was pushing a rusty, four-wheeled shopping cart which contained most of his material possessions. I remembered him immediately. It was about three years ago when I'd make the hour drive down to the Vanderbilt Clinic to see the specialist who was treating my vertigo. This same old man hung out near the Mc Donald's parking lot I would park in. I know that fast food isn't very healthy, but I've always loved Mc Donald's. I really have.

So, back then, three years ago, I'd see this old man, and I knew he was homeless and I'd always see him when I stopped at Mc Donald's near Vanderbilt. He looked very rough, as down and out as any homeless you've ever seen. What always surprised me was the fact that you'd never see him panhandling, never asking for money from the always busy stream of people entering Mc Donald's. I knew he was hungry, but I could see the pride in his eyes – he wouldn't beg. I must have seen him at least three times and it was gnawing on my heart. Here I am with plenty of money, a very well-fortified waist-line and I'd walk past him, go in Mc Donald's and eat my two quarter pounders with cheese, my large order of fries and my chocolate shake. When I came out, he'd still be there, over on the other side of the parking lot, bundled up against the weather, his pushcart nearby and even though I wouldn't look his way (couldn't), I knew he was watching me. But he never said a word, never asked for anything; he just watched me get in my car and drive away.

I thought about that old man a great deal. Who was he? What was his life about? How did he end up homeless, living on the streets of Nashville? The next time I had an appointment at the Vanderbilt Clinic, I stopped at the Mc Donald's like I always do. I walked by the old man like I always did. I avoided his eyes like I always did. I went inside and ate my fill of greasy fast food. Before I came out, I went back up to the counter and ordered three different sandwiches, two burgers and one fish as I recall. I also ordered a large chocolate shake. I asked the girl to put it in a bag to go.

When I walked out, he was where he always was, and I walked over to him. He saw me coming and I thought that maybe he looked a little uneasy. I got close to him and the bag of food was in my hand.

"Good morning, sir," I said, "I've noticed you the last several times I've been here." He didn't say anything and I know the analogy will sound stereotyped and banal, but he looked to me like the abused, neglected, beaten dog who is gun-shy to come up to you wagging his tail; instead, he cowers and drops his head in submission. "Look'" I said, "I didn't know if you were hungry or not, but I got this for you." I handed him the bag. He took it without changing the look on his face.

"Thank you," is all he said.

"I'm glad to do it. How long have you been on the streets?"

"Five years, maybe six."

"What happened?"

"I lost my job."

"No family?"

"My wife died. Two kids moved off."

"Any trouble with alcohol and drugs?"

"I drank a little. Don't no more."

"Do you ever stay at the mission?"

"Sometimes on real cold nights."

"Well ... I hope to see you again. God bless you."

"You too, mister."

That was three years ago, the day I had given the hungry, homeless man some food. That day, I had approached him. Today he was approaching me. He got up close to me, and I realized he had the warmest, most loving brown eyes I think I had ever seen. He reached back towards his rusty shopping cart and grabbed a couple of things. He didn't say anything, he just handed me a paper bag and then he grabbed my hand and shook it gently. I didn't want to say anything either. He patted my shoulder one time and then he turned to walk away. I looked quickly into the bag, looked his way, and said, "Thank you."

"I'm glad to do it. How long you been on the streets?"

"This is my fourth day."

"What happened?"

"I'm running for God."

"No family?"

"My wife's been dead for six years. My son's in Knoxville."

"You not doing any unhealthy stuff are you?"

"Quit drinking a long time ago. Same for the pot."

"You gonna' stay in the mission tonight?"

"No, I'm lucky. I'll probably be in a motel."

"Well ... I hope to see you again. God bless you."

"You too, mister," I said, and the old man started pushing his cart down the sidewalk. I opened the bag and pulled out the crackers, cheese, and one banana. I sat on the bench eating the food, and then I slipped on the tattered mittens that were in the bag. Just like Forest Gump used to say, "That's all I'm gonna' say about that."

CHAPTER 13

There was no way to avoid it. The most direct route to get through Nashville if you were on foot was to run through the lower Broadway tourist area. First, you are about a block south of the State Capital, then you are in the middle of Honky Tonk Row. Iconic landmarks like The Ryman Auditorium, Tootsies Orchard Lounge, Printers Alley, and The Ernest Tubb Record Shop mark the way. Highway 70 slips just south of the Cumberland River and in another eight miles you are as far east as Andrew Jackson's homeplace, The Hermitage.

There is certainly nothing inherently wrong with tourist areas. I understand completely they serve a valid role in our economy. They provide jobs, gathering places, entertainment, yeah, yeah. But let's face it, they aren't the best places you might choose to run in. Well, Nashville was behind me now. My thoughts were focusing on the mostly wide-open stretches of highway 70 still left between me and Knoxville. I already knew what a lot of that highway was going to look like. In the next few days, I would know what it *felt* like.

I stayed in a motel near the Hermitage that night. I talked with my son Aaron for a few minutes and also Buffalo, my neighbor. Aaron couldn't believe I had already run seventy-two miles. He kept saying that I should stop this madness immediately and that he'd come get me and take me back home. Buffalo said that Oscar seemed in a blue funk. I said take him running with you for a couple of miles. He said not to push my luck. I also dialed up 423-777-7777, but there was no signal.

The next morning started out as another cold day. I wore sweats and the tattered mittens instead of the light-weight runners gloves I had packed. The blisters were nearly gone, but still I treated them before starting to run. After I got started, I wasn't getting my breath as easily as I had been the first four days of running, not that the first four days had been easy. There was just something going on today that was a little different. The first five miles got me close to Mt. Juliet. I remember stopping for lunch at a diner and wondering if I should call off the rest of the day, find a motel and rest up until tomorrow. I didn't. I kept running. Later, about four in the afternoon I was on the outskirts of Lebanon, Tennessee when I thought I was going to puke. I got off of the shoulder of the road and went back behind a brushy fence line that also was thick with cedar trees. Instead of puking I slipped and fell to the ground. I didn't know it at the time, but I wouldn't be getting up from that spot until an hour of pure hell had elapsed.

I tried to get to my knees and almost made it, but then the "whirly- jig" took control. The whirly- jig occurs when you think planet Earth has slipped off its axis and begins spinning in the wrong direction. You think it's spinning upside down, downside up, right to left, left to right. Not only has the planet lost its sense of direction, so has everything else. You are spinning, the trees are spinning, the road is spinning, everything is spiraling and whirling in violent gyrations. Welcome to the world of vertigo. Tiny filaments in the inner ear are under siege from inflammation and infection and if you are like me, your ability to stand, walk, or run is eliminated. Classic symptoms include nausea, motion-sickness, sea-sickness, and so on.

I knew immediately what the calamitous, woeful affliction was. This wasn't my first rodeo with vertigo. After the failed attempt to get back up to my knees, I surrendered any hope that I might offset the advance of the paralysis which was sure to overwhelm me. Yep, simple as that. I gave up. I knew there was no sense fighting it. Instead of lying flat on my back, I was able to turn onto my stomach. I knew from past attacks that the head-facing-down position was the best to offset some of the terrible out of control spinning sensation which you were sure was trying to kill you. I also knew I had some meclizine tablets stowed in the first aid kit I had in my backpack. Meclizine is an effective antidote, that is, if you could get your hands on it. My meclizine tablets were strapped to my back, and in the position I was in, I couldn't get to them. Guess what? I didn't *want* to try to get to them. No sir, flat on my belly, face in the mud was where I planned on staying for at least a little while. I didn't want any part of the sickening whirly-jig that I knew would increase if I tried to get to my knees in order to remove my backpack. I was perfectly content to stay in the semi-tortuous condition I was in. I wasn't about to risk escalation into unbearable torture.

I heard someone stomping through the brush, coming my way. "Hey mister, are you okay?" It was a male voice.

"No, I'm not."

I could hear him getting really close now, but I wasn't about to try to flip over and look up at him.

"I saw you from my house, down across the road."

"I've got vertigo. I can't move. I've got medicine in my backpack." Even talking set off waves of sickening dizziness. "Look in the pack." I felt him fumbling with the pockets on my backpack.

"I see a first aid kit."

"Yeah."

"Looks like it says … it says meclizine."

"Yeah."

"How many you want?"

"Three."

"Okay, you want to try to sit up?"

"Un uh. In my mouth." He put his hand down under my mouth and I licked the three tablets out. *Just let them dissolve, then swallow the spit.*

"You want me to call an ambulance?"

"No."

"I've got my phone. I could have some help here in a couple of minutes. We're not far from town."

"No," I said. He didn't say anything but I heard him shifting around in the weeds. I guess maybe ten minutes went by. He was still there. I began to move around and then I pushed up a little and was able to sit back against a fence post. All of that brought on another round of spinning, but things weren't nearly as bad as they had been. The meclizine was kicking in.

"Are you feeling better? You want some water from your pack?"

I didn't feel like talking or moving and I knew for sure I didn't want any water, yet. Maybe in a few minutes. You gotta'

106

understand, when a big-time vertigo attack sets in, you must do one thing. Be still, don't move. There's plenty of movement going on all around you. You don't need to add to it.

I finally gathered enough courage to focus my eyes on the man. Even that slight movement nearly made me retch. But there he was, six feet away, hunched down on one knee. He looked to be around thirty. He wore camo desert fatigue pants, a black long-sleeve T with a short sleeve gray T over it, the main feature on it being a death skull and some kind of Satanic graffiti scattered around it.

"When I was in Afghanistan, we had a couple of guys with bad vertigo. We thought it was just nerves, or maybe cowards. Those guys were like you. They just couldn't move."

"Yeah," I said, "Give me a minute."

"No problem. I understand."

I sat back against the fence post, breathing slowly, remaining still. "The meclizine."

He understood and came over and removed my pack and got me three more tablets.

"Water." He got that for me too. "Thank you," I said.

"At your service. If you feel like it, what's the RFG-TIMA stand for?" I could see he was eyeing the logo on the front of my pack. I could hear cars swishing by on the highway and my stomach revolted and up came what few contents were in it.

"Meclizine," I said again. The man got me three more and some water. We sat there ten more minutes and I thought I'd make a stab at talking. "RFG means Running For God and the TIMA means This Is Man's All."

He looked confused. "You telling me you believe in God?"

"Sure I do."

"You're crazy as camel dung. You know that?"

"I don't think I'm crazy at all."

"How old are you? You ain't from around here. You got a hundred- and fifty-dollar running shoes on, good equipment, supplies, and money – I saw your billfold. What the hell are you doing? What kind of con are you into?"

"How long were you in Afghanistan?"

"Long enough to take two AK rounds through my stomach."

"I'm sorry."

"You're sorry. I guess your God's sorry too. He's sorry too, ain't he?"

"You can't put that on God."

"I'm not putting anything on God. There is no God."

"Yes there is."

"Okay, where was he when my insides came open four different times. Four times the VA said they fixed me. Four times it all opened up. You ever had a massive septic infection in your gut?"

"No, but I had one in my soul. That's pretty close."

"Yeah, yeah. And I guess your big four-star-general spirit in the sky come in and cleaned everything up."

"His Son did."

"I've heard enough." He started to walk away.

I said, "You said your house is down across the road? I'll be on my feet in thirty minutes. I'm going to stop by. I'll prove to you that God lives and that He loves you." He kept walking away and I was glad I didn't have to keep talking. I was pretty sure I would have gotten sick again.

In about twenty minutes I was able to get up on my feet. It was risky to try it, but I didn't move around. I just stood there leaning on the fence post, waiting for things to slow down and stop spinning. I remembered the first serious vertigo attack I had, and that after the E-room people gave me a shot of meclizine, it took maybe a half hour for things to slow down enough for me to get up and walk. It looked like this time it was going to be about the same.

I walked very slowly and carefully out of the brushy fence line back to the shoulder of highway 70. I saw a small house across the road and probably down about an eighth of a mile. When I got down there, I crossed the road and walked down a rutted-out driveway about fifty yards to the house. It was a wreck – everything in disrepair, junk scattered around the porch and in the yard. The roof looked like it was ready to fall. I stepped up and knocked on the door.

When he opened the door, he said, "You're wasting your time."

I said, "Can I come in?"

"You come in here, I'll shoot you."

"Okay, I'll just sit down here on the edge of your porch. You won't shoot me out here will you?"

"I don't know."

"Thank you for helping me."

It was a while before he said anything. "Old man like you shouldn't be out on the road. What are you trying to prove?"

"That's a good question. The answer is complicated. It seems like the answer changes every day."

"What do you mean?"

I slipped off the tattered mittens on my hands and held them up. "See these? Yesterday a homeless man in Nashville gave these to me. Two days before that a jail chaplain in Dickson County took me to the jail to speak to some prisoners. A couple of days before that I watched as God prevented a man from committing suicide. The very next day the man's wife tried doing the same thing, but God was with me and helped me stop her. You see what I mean? It's complicated."

"I don't get it."

"*You* don't get it? You want to hear the real kicker?"

"What do you mean?"

"I mean, do you want to hear the craziest thing that has happened to me in the last twelve days?"

"I don't know."

"Well … you either want to hear it or you don't."

"Yeah, I guess so."

"Okay. Did you know that area code 423 is from the mountains in east Tennessee?"

"Yeah, so what?"

"I've been getting calls from God from that area code."

He shook his head like there was no hope for me, or for him. I thought maybe he'd get his gun.

Before I knew it, I was pulling my phone out of my pack. I said, "I can see you don't believe me. Look at this." I pulled up the call log and highlighted the incoming 423-777-7777 calls. "See, I told you."

I could tell that when he saw the phone number on the screen that it triggered some kind of recognition in his brain. Something in there said, "Whoa!", but he didn't say anything. I looked at him not like his fifth-grade teacher might have, but as a buddy sharing a fox hole might have. "Hey, your turn. Tell me what that stuff on your T-shirt is about."

"Just some stuff I mess around with, that's all."

"Just stuff you mess around with, huh? So, you know what the seven sevens mean?"

"I know what some people probably think it means."

What I was about to say wasn't thought out, but you know me. I go ahead and say it anyway. "Remember, I told you I could prove that there is a God and that He loves you. Remember?" He stayed quiet. "Why don't you dial Him up? There's the number, right there. I bet you feel like you can dial up Satan anytime you want. I'm telling you to dial up God."

"You are an absolutely certified psycho."

"You chicken? You afraid He will answer?"

"Give me the phone," he said. I handed it to him and watched as he hit the call icon for the highlighted 423-777-7777.

"Put the speaker on. I want to hear this." He flicked it on.

After two rings the British voice sounded cheery and efficient, just like he always did. "Beyond Time – Before Creation, may I help you?"

"Cute. Who is this?" He smiled as if this was the best joke he'd heard in a long time.

"Sir, I am the receptionist. Would you like to speak to someone in authority?"

"Someone in authority, eh? I thought this was supposed to be God's number. You people couldn't fake out a children's third grade Sunday school class."

"Please hold, sir."

The next voice that came over the speaker was the older Appalachian mountain voice. "Well, well, it's good to hear from you, Lenny. I was hoping you'd give me a call. I know Coach Finn is there with you. Why don't you tell him what you were really going to do with your gun just a few minutes ago? You can trust Coach Finn, he's one of our counsellors."

That was it. The line went dead. Lenny held the phone out in front of him and stared at it before handing it back to me. Then he gave me the same stare.

"I know," I said, "He does the same thing to me."

"But, I … I, uh, I can't …" His words bled away to vapor.

"Look, we can talk about it all we want. It'll take a while to settle in. But there's something we should do first – *you* should do first." He gave me another totally blank stare. I said, "Do you smoke?" I was looking at his yellow fingers. He shook his head, yes. I said, "Do you have a lighter on you?" He shook his head again. "Why don't you take off that T-shirt and burn it. Right here, right now. Just burn it."

"But …"

"Tell me if I'm wrong, okay? You always hear my side talking about the "free will" God's given us, right? Now it is your chance. Look, the leader of your side never gives his followers a choice, does he? Be honest. He never gives a choice. It's always his total dominance, isn't it? There's no room to weigh both sides, is there?" I shut up.

"Get out of here." His empty eyes looked lost.

"Lenny. Is that short for Leonard"

"I said get out of here." His eyes didn't look empty that time. I got moving, headed down the road.

CHAPTER 14

Four miles later I found a motel on the east side of Lebanon, Tennessee. The town was started in 1801 and with a current population of 34,000, I guess you could say it hasn't really grown very much. It was named after the "cedars of Lebanon" from the Old Testament and in modern days proudly claims the best county fair in Tennessee – The Wilson County Fair.

Before crashing on the bed in my room, I took two more meclizine tablets. From past experience, I knew I would be taking at least one tablet a day for a couple of weeks. That's just the way it rolls. I'd have to be very careful in order to avoid another major attack. And, that night I was a basket case. No going across the street for a meal. I'd have to make do with rations from my backpack.

I'd been resting on the bed for three hours; sleep was a luxury that bypassed me. I was thinking a lot about Lenny – worrying a lot about Lenny. My cell phone went off. I picked up.

"Hello."

"Coach Finn, this is Lenny. How are you feeling?"

"I'm feeling much better. How are you doing?"

"That's why I called. I hope you don't mind, I took a peek at your number when I had your phone, to, uh … you know, to call …"

"To call God," I said.

"Uh, yeah, I'm trying to figure it out," Lenny said. I didn't respond. Sometimes it's better to hang low.

A long silence ensued, then, "Coach Finn, you still there?"

"Yeah, Lenny, I'm right here."

"Okay, look, uh … I burned the T-shirt. You were right, Satan never gives you a chance. It's always condemnation, guilt, and hate. Would you accept my apology, I mean, you know, for the way I treated you?"

"Lenny, it's not about you and me. Don't get me wrong. Sure, I accept your apology, but it's really about you and the Father. It's about accepting the sacrifice His Son, Jesus, made for you on the cross."

"Do you know what I was about to do when you knocked on my door?"

"No."

"I was going to kill myself."

"That would have been a terrible sin."

"I was a second away from pulling the trigger. You must be an angel. You saved me."

"I'm no angel. I'm just a lost sinner."

"Whatever you are, I'm grateful."

The next morning I was up at sunrise and in the lobby of the motel. How these people call granola, fruit, and yogurt a real breakfast, I'd never know. But at least they had plenty of coffee. Some people declare wine as the nectar of the Gods. Not me. I'll take good fresh coffee – thank you very much.

Lingering dizziness showed up again, but I swallowed enough meclizine tablets to wake up a Rocky Mountain Grizzly in hibernation. I did not know what hazards and perils might be in store for me on this new day, but I was ready to find out. I was running for God, that was man's all. That was *my* all. I trotted off down the shoulder of the highway acting more like a twenty-year-old than a sixty-eight-year-old who could barely maintain enough balance to stay on his feet. Things got better as the day wore on. One mile under my belt. Then two miles, then three. Four miles and I'd have to say there was very little dizziness. The hill country was seriously into late fall. Blazing color surrounded me. In flat stretches of the highway, I could see the land to my east rising and falling and rising again into the loftier climbs of the Cumberland Plateau. Oh boy, there were real inclines waiting for me in the next couple of days.

At about 12 miles I came to what truck drivers call a "Mom and Pop pullover", not a real truck stop that now days offers at least two restaurants, barbers, church services, etc. and could easily park two hundred tractor-trailers. No, a "Mom and Pop pullover" was lucky to have enough room to squeeze in maybe four or five big trucks, a lot of times around back where the potholes were big enough to swallow a Saint Bernard. The sign on the place said, "Peppers Whole Hog Bar B Q – Best In Tennessee." I was inside quicker than a frog snatching a fly.

Needless to say, about the only way a stranger can really tell whether or not an out of the way country Bar B Q joint would be any good, is to count how many vehicles are parked outside. This place had a lot – at least twenty. Three of the vehicles were the monster tractor-trailers that dominate the interstate highway

115

system. It's estimated that at any given time there are eight billion, five hundred million pounds of freight being transported over American highways. That shakes out at four million, two hundred and fifty thousand tons. That's only freight hauled by eighteen-wheelers. If you included smaller trucks you would probably come close to doubling those numbers. The trucking industry likes to say, if you own it, a truck brought it. Fifty years ago, truck drivers were described as "Knights of the highway". The good deeds and helping hands they provided to the driving public was legendary. Modern times has seen their image deteriorate to much lower standards, sometimes including irresponsible drifters often the targets of serial rape and murder investigations.

So, anyway, I'm walking into the Bar B Q joint and I took particular notice of one of the three eighteen-wheelers parked outside. Two of the trucks were specialty type vehicles. One was an auto-hauler, commonly referred to by truckers as "parking lots". The other was a flatbed. The moniker flatbeds went by was "skateboards". Funny, I guess, the third truck, the one that caught my attention, was a common box trailer. But it wasn't the trailer I was looking at, it was the words custom painted on the door of the tractor, "JETS – Jesus Express Truckers", and the driver's name right below – Jabez. I went inside and took a seat at an empty table by a window.

"Hi Darlin'. What can I get you today?" Brenda was my waitress. I know because her name was on her shirt. A pig's picture was on her shirt too, and there were words stenciled in next to it that said, "I'm Porky, this is Brenda." Brenda's mouth was working steadily on a wad of gum, but that didn't interfere with the big smile she threw around at anybody that cared to notice.

"Brenda, I bet you folks don't have a special today," I said.

"Why sure we do, Darlin'. Look right up there." She pointed to a nearby wall with a menu board on it. The special was a pulled pork sandwich, barbecued beans, coleslaw, pie, and a drink.

I said, "You know what? Just shoot me the special. Make the drink coffee, and the pie, make it Pecan."

"You got it, Sweety."

"And Brenda, don't ever stop that pretty smile."

"Aw, Honey, you beat all."

Once, a sage said that you knew you were in the south when you saw a Cadillac headed for the river with a bunch of cane fishing poles sticking out the windows. I might add to that the Burma Shave signs along the highway, or the Wigwam Village on the Dixie Highway in Kentucky, or the "See Rock City" signs on the sides of countless barns. Eating my barbecue sandwich, I was thinking here's another sure sign that you're in the south – waitresses like Brenda.

Another thing I was thinking … wondering … was which of the three truckers perched on stools up at the counter was the trucker that belonged to the truck outside which had the name Jabez painted on the door? Their backs were toward me, so I couldn't really see what they looked like. Two of them paid their bill and left but there was nothing in their countenance that would have tied them to the truck in question. The riddle was solved a few minutes later when the third driver turned toward the door to leave. He wore a ball cap with the words "Hammer Down, Heaven Bound" across the front.

Was he the truck driver with the name Jabez? I was thinking he was. And so what? What was so special about that name? What was it that lured my attention towards it? For one thing, it

117

was biblical. I was certain of that. But I couldn't recall where in the Bible it appeared, or what role the character, Jabez, might have played in some biblical story.

As the driver was leaving, he gave me a quick nod and then he tipped his ball cap, you know, the way the leader of the final two golfers do to the crowd gathered around the 18th green on Sunday at the Masters. He left the Bar B Q joint and I looked out the window. I paid close attention as the driver crossed the parking lot and climbed the two safety steps to enter his truck. Sure enough, when the door closed behind him, I saw the same words I'd seen before – JETS, JESUS EXPRESS TRUCKERS, and JABEZ.

While I was eating my lunch, I googled the name Jabez and was quickly led to 1 Chronicles in the Old Testament. Chapter 4, verse 10 reads as follows:

"And Jabez called on the God of Israel saying, 'Oh, that You would bless me indeed, and enlarge my territory, that Your hand would be with me, and that You would keep me from evil, that I may not cause pain!' So God granted him what he requested."

Another brain tease, freeze, squeeze? Why had the truck driver nodded my way and tipped his cap? I had no idea. I saw Brenda coming my way. "Hey Brenda, do you know that man that just left?"

"No sweetheart, don't believe I've seen him before. He'd sure get your attention though."

"You mean his ball cap?" I said.

"Yeah, I guess. But did you notice how old he looked?"

She was right. I'd guess he was a good stretch beyond eighty, but he moved like a much younger man; just had a presence about him.

The afternoon would soon slip away and leave me with a mileage deficit if I didn't get moving. Reluctantly I got up to leave the warm surroundings of Pepper's. I left Brenda a healthy tip and a hardy, "God Bless you, Darlin'."

"You too, Hon." Magnificent.

About six miles later I wrapped up another eighteen- mile running day. I was in a motel at a little place called Carthage. It is on the banks of the Cumberland River and as far as I know owns no notoriety other than being the boyhood home of Al Gore Jr.

The dizziness from the vertigo seemed to have vanished, but just like I remember from years past, you couldn't be sure it wouldn't return at any time. Think of an airplane on instrument control. Were you really on the horizontal pitch you needed to be? You sure couldn't tell by looking out the windshield – nothing but a gray cloudy obscurity, no sense of azimuth or stability. Oh well, there was nothing I could do about it. Just keep popping the meclizine tablets. And keep praying that this new existence of mine was what God really wanted me to do. I sort of had a feeling that once I started following the signs, that it was all out of my control anyway.

Sleep came easy that night and then a couple of hours before sun-up, the dreams started. I saw soldiers in far-off lands. I saw explorers and adventurers scaling icy mountain cliffs. I saw sailors and seamen under triple masted sail, skimming the aqua blue seas of Polynesia. The last things I saw before awaking were big trucks. Trucks of all kinds moving across a worried continent which was occupied by worried inhabitants. The drivers were resolute, dauntless, bound and determined to deliver their loads on time. My focus narrowed down to one particular tractor pulling a box van. Painted on its door was

119

JETS, JESUS EXPRESS TRUCKERS, and JABEZ. I could see inside the cab. An older than dirt truck driver was at the wheel. A dog was on the floor ripping and tearing a plastic toy that looked like the devil. The dog had a collar around his neck with the name Nicodemus on it. I thought maybe the dream was over, but the truck driver reached for his CB microphone and as he keyed it, I heard him say in that now familiar Appalachian accent, "What's your twenty, driver?"

An unfamiliar voice answered up; a voice I could only assume was another truck driver who was about to answer the question the old man had asked him. "I'm up here on top Mont Eagle, west bound, heading for St. Louis."

"Ten-four driver. I reckon we got about eight hours in front of us. I'm headed that way too."

"Okay, I thought we must be headed the same way, 'cause I've been picking up your signal, on and off, for the last half hour. Was that you singing a few minutes ago?"

"No, I believe that feller was going back towards Atlanta, but I know the song he was singing."

"You do? It sounded like that old trucker song the JETS used to sing out here."

The Appalachian voice came back, "That's the one all right."

"I believe they used to call it *Open Highway.*"

The Appalachian trucker said, "Yessir, I think you're right."

"Do you know it good enough to sing it?"

"I reckon I could give it a try."

The dream stalled for a moment. I had no idea a dream could contain the lyrics to a song, but this one certainly did. I listened as the song started out:

Open highway, open highway, I hear your call
Like an angry old lover, you wanted my all
Well, I'll give you what I got, but it ain't very much
Jesus my Savior, now he's my real crutch

Now I started truck drivin' to see if I could
Now I'm driving forever, I knew that I would
Open highway, open highway, you've tortured my soul
You've run me through this land, so that's where I'll go

Yes, I'll die on your pavement and if they will fit
My brakes and my drive shaft, right there they will sit
But my soul's going to heaven, not to your big road
Jesus my Savior will carry my load

Now they say that truck drivers are modern cowboys
They lead a rough life, but that is their choice
And they say that the cowboys all ride to be free
And truck drivers are sailors on that big concrete sea

Now truck drivers and cowboys they like to roam
But only Dear Jesus can show their way home
Yes only Dear Jesus can show their way home

The song was over and as soon as it was, I woke up from the
dream, although the mood and the feelings it had stirred in me
would continue most of the morning. Is that what it felt like to
be an over-the-road, long distance truck driver? Whew! Heavy
stuff. I knew one thing. I didn't want to spend time trying to
connect the dots, you know, the real-life trucker I'd seen earlier
that day and the dream trucker with the same name painted on

his door who sang as if he and that "open highway" were one; as if human being and paved roadway were inseparable, at least until death. You had the feeling that living in and driving a truck was the actual blood flowing through the singer's veins.

CHAPTER 15

On that note I awoke to a new day of running – my seventh straight day of eighteen miles a day. I took an assessment of my situation – my physical condition as well as my mental condition. Remember the old hippie song, *I Just Dropped In To See What Condition My Condition Was In*? I always liked that song. The first thing I wanted to check on was my weight. Like the last time, I called on the motel manager to borrow his scales. I was down to 225. I had started this eighteen mile-a-day madness at 250. So I was losing an average of a little over four pounds a day. I could live with that – well, for a while anyway. The next thing I checked were the blisters. No problems there. The painful pus-filled bubbles had become tough, leathery skin. How about the vertigo? I've already described it more than enough. It was what it was, and I wasn't going to change it. What about my energy level and my general state of mind? I'd have to say, that was what I felt the best about. None of the strange events, not even the mystery of the 423-777-7777 phone calls had rattled me enough to shake or to change my conviction that what I was doing was what I was supposed to be doing. And let me tell you, neighbor, when you are doing what you are supposed to be doing, things aren't complicated. Things fit. Things work out. You may not be seeing the entire big picture without some fuzziness in it, but you see enough of it to know you're going in the direction you need to be going in.

That was good enough for me. I had breakfast that morning and after having started out at a very slow jog. I gradually picked up my pace. Five miles later I'd bet I was running at under nine-minute-miles, something I hadn't done in years. Was it possible, I was thinking, could I possibly lower that down to an eight-minute-mile? I was going to find out. The highway I was on had the one- mile markers pegged along the shoulder. The next peg I came to I started the stopwatch mode on my runner's watch. One mile later I looked down at my watch; it read seven minutes and forty-nine seconds. I'd done it – ran a sub eight-minute mile. What a day! Sixty -eight years old and I'm running at a pace most forty-year-olds would be proud of. I had enough gumption to slow it down the rest of the day. What was I trying to prove? It was fun, that's all. It was just one of those things you know could hurt you, but … hey, you only live once. That night in the motel, as I was praying, I was very thankful that the Lord saw fit to let an old man be out here running for Him, and allowing that old man a sub eight-minute mile. What an awesome God was the God I loved, the God I was running for.

Two days later I found myself still running on Highway 70, just east of Monterey. Knoxville was still eighty miles away. Some of the grades I had to climb were steep enough that I walked a lot of them. I didn't have any fun on them, wasn't trying to prove anything either – just trying to survive. Still, it was a great feeling, running in the heights of the Cumberland Plateau, running for God because it was man's all. Certainly, it was *my* all.

I saw a car a hundred yards in front of me; it was pulled off the road in a wide grassy area. The closer I got I could see it was empty, but a woman was standing outside. I just had a feeling that she was in trouble. I walked up towards her, maybe ten feet away, "Your car break down?"

"Nunh uh."

I knew something was wrong. She was by herself. She was pulled over out here on this lonely stretch, just standing there. I'd say she was forty or so. She was plain, but pleasantly plain. I guess most men's initial appraisal of a woman usually grades the curves first, or lack there-of. I don't think I'm any different. This woman had all the curves, but she also had a much more ordinary feature, a sort of shroud around her that obscured the feminine attributes.

"Are you waiting for someone?"

"No." She only vaguely glanced my way.

"Well, I guess if you are all right, I'll just …" I couldn't just keep going. "Listen, if you could tell me what it is maybe I could help."

She looked right at me this time, but just for a second. "Nah, that's okay."

"Could you at least tell me why you're out here? I mean, maybe there's something I could do."

"Nah, I better go." But she didn't move towards her car.

"Where you going?"

"I don't know."

"Hey, sit down for a minute before you go. You don't have to tell me anything." I gestured towards the hood of her car. She didn't move. I walked over and dropped my bottom on the edge of the hood. "Sit down," I said, "Just for a minute." Several cars whizzed by out on the highway. She looked my way and took a step closer but didn't come to the hood.

"I'm a grandfather. I'm on my way to Knoxville to see my son and his family. They've got three kids. You know, if any of them were in some kind of trouble, I'd love to see somebody stop and check on them." That's all I said to her. She didn't say anything, but after a moment or so, she sat down on the hood next to me. We didn't talk at all.

I guess it was about ten minutes, she got up and stepped around towards the door to her car and said, "I gotta' go. Thank you."

That night I chose a motel on the west side of Crossville. As I was walking from the road to the entrance driveway, I noticed a big eighteen-wheeler barreling down the highway. I couldn't read anything on the truck's door, but the resemblance to the truck I saw a driver named Jabez climb into a few days ago was undeniable. I was too tuckered out to even think about it.

After checking in and finding my room, I wolfed down two cans of sardines I had in my backpack along with a triple layered peanut butter sandwich I made and also a pack of beef jerky. I crashed on the bed and didn't move for two hours. When I got up, I went to the pool, swam a couple of laps, but mostly just let the heated water work on my overworked muscles. When I got back to the room, I started eating again. This time I worked on apples, oranges, celery, strawberries, and blueberries. I'd picked up those wonderful items at a market across the street from the motel. I felt like I'd be fortified, fueled- up and ready to go for tomorrow. Protein, omega three, fat, fiber, anti-oxidants, and plenty of vitamin C would get me off to a good start tomorrow morning. Three more solid days of eighteen milers would get me to the western side of Knoxville. That's where my son Aaron was, and I was getting excited to see him and his family.

Thinking about what would lie ahead once I got to Knoxville, my thoughts drifted back to my Christian counselling clients, Renae Holsclaw, and of course Justin Barkley and his wife, Julie. I picked up my phone and called Renae.

"Hey Coach Finn, I thought maybe you forgot about me."

"Oh no, I haven't forgotten. I'll be back in time for your sentencing hearing. It's Monday morning, right?"

Oh no, Renae thought, *how can I tell him?* "Coach Finn, there won't be a hearing Monday morning."

"No hearing. Why not? What's happened?"

"Uh, something happened four days ago,"

I didn't like the sound of that. "Okay," I said and waited for her to spill the beans.

"I guess I should have known better. You see … my old boyfriend called me. He said he'd overdosed and he needed help. I told him I couldn't get involved with drugs, you know … but he really sounded in bad shape, so I went over there." She stopped.

"Go on," I said.

"Well, when I got there, two of his buddies were there and a girl. They were having a party. Derrick wasn't OD'd. He just faked that to get me over there. They were drinking and smoking and I wanted to leave, but they wouldn't let me." She stopped again.

"They wouldn't let you?"

"No sir. I swear."

"I see. Let me guess. I bet the cops showed up and you all went to jail."

"Yeah, and the next day, the only reason I got out, was because they said the judge granted me a week to find a place for my daughter. I don't know what I'm gonna' do. My public defender says I'm going back to jail no matter what. He says he can't see how I won't be convicted on a fourth drug charge and that I'm looking at one year in prison at the least."

"Renae, this is terrible."

"I know." She sounded lower than a snake's belly.

"Do you have any prospects for taking care of your baby?"

"No sir. I've tried. My aunt who took Wendy the last time, she's sick, in and out of the hospital."

"Keep trying. Don't give up. And look, if you haven't been praying, I'd say now would be a good time to start."

"Yes sir."

I felt bad. I was thinking that if I hadn't hit the road, if I had remained in the Clarksville area, maybe there was something I could have done. I went to the Lord with prayer that somehow a resolution would come forth, an answer to the looming reality that Renae was about to lose her daughter.

My next call was to Justin Barkley. I was hoping there would be no bad news from that quarter.

"Hello."

"Justin, this is Finn Weaver. I'm calling to see how you and Julie have been doing."

"We are doing much better. We'd like to see you again. You've been a big help. We're kind of wondering what the next step ought to be?"

"Okay, I'm out of town now, but I'll be back in four days. I'll call when I get in. Will that be all right – we set something up then?"

"Yes, that'll be good. There's something else."

"Shoot."

"We haven't received a bill from you."

"Justin, you're not going to receive a bill from me. I started my Christian Counselling Service to give back. I'm in it to serve God, to put my hand out to someone who might need it."

"You know, I remember that you told us, you told Julie and me, that we were only your second case. There was a young woman I believe. Something about a young woman and her child."

"Yes, that's right. She's about to lose custody of her baby to the state. That's ... oops ... sorry, I should not have mentioned that."

"I understand." There was a long pause before He came back. "I'm thinking there's ... uh, you know I told you Julie and I are wandering what the next step might be for us."

"Yes, I heard you say that."

"Do you think you could give us that young woman's number?"

CHAPTER 16

The Bible tells us that God is spirit and that God works in mysterious ways. After last night's two phone calls, I could think of no reason to think otherwise.

It was time to "saddle up" as the infantry grunts in Vietnam used to say – time to start "humping" the jungle trails. In my case, that morning, it was time to run. I ate what little fruit I had left over from last night, and then I ambushed the motel lobby's sad collection of breakfast choices. One thing they *did* have, and it was the first time I'd seen this, was hard-boiled eggs. There were ten of them in the bowl. I ate six, and then tried to avoid the eyes of five or six other guests.

Still eastbound on Highway 70, the road was a continuous downhill grade, five or six miles to the valley below. The tiny town of Crab Orchard was down there. I spotted a small store with gas pumps out front and almost decided to go in and purchase a Gatorade, but I didn't. The running down the slope had been spectacular. Crisp and cool, the morning air was a seductive teaser, a beguiling temptress, asking me to shoot for a seven-minute mile. I knew better. I was content to amble along and simply enjoy the natural beauty of the mountains around me. One of those mountains was Big Rock Mountain. It dwarfed the surrounding landscape and controlled most of the vista north of the little town. I could see railroad tracks east of the mountain winding their way down to some kind of heavy industrial site at the base of the mountain. It was a mine. You could see three entrances cut right into the side of the mountain. There were large buildings down below the entrance tunnels. There were loading docks, both for rail and trucks. There were enormous mounds of crushed rock and aggregate rock. Heavy equipment of every kind was busy, working all around the complex.

Coming into Crab Orchard there was a sign stating the population was 1,406. Coming out of Crab Orchard, one minute later, I could see that the eastbound highway snuggled right up to the entrance to the mine property. The morning was warming up. I had already run about seven miles; I needed hydration. I looked in my pack for my water bottle and found it empty. I had forgotten to refill it before leaving the motel. Now I wished I had stopped at the store to pick up some Gatorade, but I wasn't about to turn around and run back. I was getting close to the turn off from Highway 70 into the mine property. Maybe fifty yards in I saw a small building which served as the scale house for trucks as well as the general office for the mine. There must have been fifteen or twenty pick-up trucks parked off to the east side of the building. I needed some water; I thought why not go in and beg a little water from a tap in the building? That's what I did.

The building was about the size of any modest home. It was covered in a fine, sandy dust as was every square inch of the entire property. Many of the workers I could see outside wore masks. I went inside via the front door which didn't look like it received a lot of traffic. I assumed, correctly, that most of the employees used a back entrance. There were four men inside, only one of whom wasn't covered head to toe in the same powdery silica dust I'd seen outside. Two of them wore those miner's hard hats with the little light on the front. One wore a Redman Tobacco ball cap, and you could see the black stain of tobacco juice driveling from his mouth leaving its mark on his salt and pepper four-day beard stubble. The fourth man probably ran the office. He was sitting behind a metallic desk strewn with paperwork, walkie talkies, and some small hand tools.

I said, "I've come to beg a little water." I held up my empty water jug so they could see it.

They searched me up and down and finally one of them said, "Where's your pants, mister?"

I had removed my sweats earlier in the morning about halfway down that slope coming out of the motel. "On good days, I usually just run in shorts."

"I'll be." It was the same man. "You one of them Yankees from up to Fairfield Glade?"

"Me? No, no. I'm from Clarksville."

"Clarksville? That'd be up the other side of Nashville. What'a you doin' out here with no pants on?"

Oh boy, I was thinking. *All four of them looked like they'd stepped out of the movie Deliverance. And they weren't the city boys from Atlanta to do a little river canoeing. No, they were*

the broken toothed, back-woods hayseeds that would like to get
you alone for five minutes.

I looked around at all four of them. I thought I'd see a little grin, maybe a quick laugh. I didn't see that. Their faces were like stone, their eyes dead.

"He asked you a question, mister."

"Look," I said, "I can get my water some place else." I started to turn for the door.

"Not so fast, mister." One of them got between me and the door. "We asked you a question. You too good for our kind? What's that on your shirt? RFG-TIMA?"

"Leave him be, Bubba. I don't think he means nothin'. He ain't from around here." It was the man from the desk. "Mister, you gotta' understand. We ain't never seen somebody like you come in here off the highway. I mean people around here don't go a runnin' around in their underwear."

"Okay," I said, "I can understand that. Get Bubba out of the way and I'll tell you what the RFG-TIMA means."

"Move over, Bubba." Bubba slid away a few feet, leaving an unobstructed path to the door. "RFG-TIMA means Running For God – This Is Man's All. That's what I'm doing out here. I've been doing it every day. It's been about nine days since I left Clarksville."

"Are you saying to me, mister, that you're a man of God?"

"I'm trying to follow Him the best I know how. This is what He's told me to do."

You could sense a different vibe spring up. One of the others, not Bubba, not the desk-man, came closer to me and was mining my eyes. "We got us a little church 'bout five mile from here, ya' know. We meet every Sunday, 'cept the fourth Sunday. That's when we all pack up and go up to the Kentucky

134

line for a special service at our sister church. You wanta' see what we take with us when we go up there?"

"Sure."

He went into a back room and returned with a wooden box with screened ventilation holes on the sides. The box was about a three- foot square, three foot high, and had a solid wooden lid which fit firmly on the top. He placed the box on a table and said, "Open it up."

I was thinking, *wait a minute, Finn,* but something else said, *go ahead and open it.* I did.

The first thing that happened was the sharp, medium pitched rattle I heard. It was like a handful of dry little seashells were in your hands and you were shaking them. Then I saw on the bottom of the box, three snakes. I guess I don't have to tell you what kind of snakes they were.

"Your church is Pentecostal, right?"

"Sometimes we call it The Tabernacle of God."

"You go to Kentucky because it's illegal to own venomous snakes in Tennessee."

"Yeah. The law gets on us sometimes, so we go up there."

"The Gospel of Mark: 'And these signs will follow those who believe. In My name they will cast out demons; they will speak with new tongues; they will take up serpents; and if they drink anything deadly, it will by no means hurt them; they will lay hands on the sick and they will recover.'"

"I guess maybe we misread you mister. Are you one of us?"

"No, I'm a Methodist. I've never handled snakes. Not in a religious ceremony, or any other time."

"Well, I reckon you could if you want to. We've got three gooduns' right here."

At first, I thought maybe it was a dare. I thought maybe it was some kind of privative, recusant pressure on me to handle the snakes. But that's not what it was at all. It was a sincere offer, gift, if you will, an opportunity these men were giving me to get right with God.

I wanted to be careful; to choose my words wisely. I also wanted to be truthful. "Thank you, but I believe you'd agree with me, the Spirit must call you. Believe me, if I felt The Holy Spirit calling on me to handle serpents, I believe I would. It's just that He's called on me to do other things, and that's what I'm trying to do."

"Well," the man at the desk said, "You probably want to be getting' on your way." He walked across the room to a cooler, reached in and pulled out a 32-ounce plastic bottled water and brought it over to me.

As I was walking down the entrance driveway out of the mine property, I was thinking how thirsty I was and how good that water was going to taste.

But wait. I stopped walking and looked back over my shoulder. Then I turned around and stood there staring at a loading-dock down at the end of a warehouse. I could see a forklift loading a box trailer with skids of bagged, crushed rock. I looked to the tractor and thought I recognized it, but then another big truck backed in next to it and I couldn't see it anymore.

That night was a restless orgy of fitful dreams. Surprisingly there were no snakes. There were zebras and African antelope. There were crowds of people. I couldn't determine who they were or where they were. And there was an unsettling sequence of a man using an old fashioned, rotary dial telephone receiver. He was trying to call someone and the call never went through.

He kept dialing, and dialing, and dialing, but there was no response on the other end. When I woke up, I felt exhausted.

The next two days of running carried me all the way to Aaron's house in the western suburbs of Knoxville. I met some interesting people along the way and was able to have good conversations with three or four of them. One lady in a truck stop was taken by the tattered mittens I wore when I entered the truck stop. I had taken them off of course and laid them on the table when I sat down in the Mc Donald's to enjoy my lunch of three Big Macs, a chocolate shake, and large fries. Oh yeah, add three coffees to that.

She walked over and was looking at the mittens and then she looked at me. "I know those mittens." She was a rosy-cheeked grandmotherly lady. She was warm and special.

I said, "Now don't tell me you made them."

"I certainly did. Look inside, you'll see my son's initials stitched in a red and gray double -cross-stitch."

I looked inside, "I'll be. I've never noticed that. I've only had them six or seven days. Would you care to sit down?"

"Well … I …uh …" I could see she was considering what it might look like for a lady to join a perfect stranger at a truck stop.

"I assure you; I only have honorable motives and it appears to me that this looks like a mystery worthy of investigating."

"Well, maybe for a minute."

"I'm Finn weaver."

"I'm Margie Babb. It's nice to meet you."

"Yes Ma'am, same here. Like I said, I've only had these mittens, let me see … it was eight days ago. An old homeless man in Nashville gave them to me."

"I'm on my way to North Carolina to see my grand babies. I've got mittens and socks I knitted for them."

"You sound like you keep yourself busy."

"You know what they say, 'Idle hands are the devil's workshop.'"

"I haven't heard that in a while. It's nice to know that someone still remembers it."

"I sure do. Now, Mr. Weaver, let me tell you about these mittens. I guess it was about five years ago. I made them for my son, Robert James Babb. You see those initials are RJB."

"Yes Ma'am, they sure are."

"Well, it was winter, you see. I do most of my knitting in cold weather. I'm always in the garden or canning in warm weather."

"Yes Ma'am, I understand."

"I made them up for Robert, and you know, he's the one that lives in North Carolina."

"Yes Ma'am."

"I probably shouldn't have tried to drive over there in the winter time, but I did. It was on the other side of Knoxville. I think it's what they call the "Gorge", you know, way up in the mountains. Well, people said it was the snow that caused it. Rocks, no, not rocks … boulders, trees, snow, you name it, started sliding down towards the interstate. I would have got covered up. But you know, what happened was, a trucker pulled his rig out around me and took most of that slide. He saved my life. He was pinned in his truck. It took four hours to get him out. I'll never forget it. I guess I could have left, but I didn't. I waited until they got him out. I didn't have much with me, but I did have those mittens for Robert. I gave them to that truck driver. He wasn't hurt bad. He saved my life, so I gave those mittens to him."

"That was mighty kind of you, Miss Babb. And that was five years ago?"

"Yes sir. Five years ago."

"The only mystery left is how they got from the trucker to the homeless man."

"I doubt there's much mystery there," she said.

"What do you mean?"

"You'd have to see that trucker to know what I mean. He was like an angel, Mr. Weaver. I don't think I've ever seen anybody with eyes like his. They twinkled like stars, Mr. Weaver. You could see the love in that man. He saved my life, you know, evidently with no concern about the risk to his own life. I'm sure, one cold day, he was driving along in Nashville and saw the homeless man, and he gave those mittens to him."

"Do you remember anything else about the trucker?"

"Why sure. I'll never forget him. He was the oldest truck driver I've ever seen. And that hat he wore. I thought it was perfect for him."

"What do you mean?"

"His ball cap said, 'Hammer Down, Heaven Bound.'"

CHAPTER 17

It was almost 7 PM on Saturday night as I walked along the street in the development where my son Aaron's house was. As I stated earlier, I'm reluctant to describe these kinds of neighborhoods as subdivisions, although technically that's what they are. When I was growing up back in the sixties, fifteen houses were jammed into maybe two and a half acres. The square lots from let's say "a bird's eye view", looked like a checkerboard. There was practically no deviation in the designs of the homes. They were cookie cutter houses with different shades of paint or brick; that was all. My dad's generation, coming out of WW II was glad to have one of these invariable and uniform dwellings to raise their families in. The male offspring of these men played war in the backyards and the surrounding fields. They didn't know they were rehearsing their own devastation and tragedy that would soon be played out in the jungles and rice paddies of Vietnam, but they were.

The kids I grew up with in small subdivision America would have called Aaron's house a mansion. Aaron wouldn't. But he was proud of it, and he had a right to be. He was a good kid. He'd always worked for what he had. He had played on some of the basketball teams I had coached, but he wasn't treated any differently from the other players. He was awarded playing time based on what he could contribute to the team effort – nothing more. But I love him as if he is the only kid I have. That's because he is.

Aaron's wife, Crystal, answered the door when I rang the bell. "Coach Finn, we've been expecting you." She gave me a little squeeze and brought me inside. "Aaron's upstairs in his office, I'll get him. Girls, your grandad is here."

My three granddaughters banged through the house and jumped on me. Aaron came down and the first thing he said after looking me over was, "Where's the rest of you?"

"I left a little out on the road. Come here." I put a wrap-around hug on him. "You ought to try it. It'll do wonders for your constitution, not to mention your regularity."

"We thought you were nuts. Did you run the whole way?"

"Most of it."

"Are you hungry?"

"Who, me?"

We ate and talked until eleven. The girls had gone down about nine. Aaron had asked me if there was any adventure in the trip? I lied and said not much. Crystal asked me if I'd met any interesting women. I said I'd met one very sweet grandmother. I told them about the mittens and they just went back to the "We think you're nuts" theory, but they said that's why they loved me so much. I said I felt like at least there's *some* reason they love me. We all laughed.

142

I went to church with them Sunday morning and after that, Aaron and I started on the four-hour drive back to Clarksville. We talked a little basketball, mostly about how the Austin Peay Governors and the Tennessee Volunteers might fare in the new season. We talked about the girls and a little about what kind of world might be waiting for them when they became adults. That scared the starch out of us and I was obliged to remind Aaron that if the girls found Jesus on the way to adulthood, that their eternal destinies were guaranteed to be faultless, unblemished, incorruptible, immaculate, virtuous, and saintly – in short, Holy. He gave me a nod and said, "I love you, Dad." I said, "I love you, son."

When we got as far west as Crab Orchard, I said, "See that mining operation over there on the side of the mountain?" We were whizzing along the interstate at seventy-five, but the view of Big Rock Mountain was unobstructed.

Aaron said, "Sure. Look, you can see three tunnels dug into the side. I've always wondered what kind of a mine that place was."

"Mostly crushed rock and aggregate, I believe. See the small building down there at the bottom, near the entrance, off highway 70?"

"Yeah, so?"

"Oh nothing. I was just thinking about it. I stopped in there the other day. I was out of water and they gave me a 32-ounce, chilled water bottle. Surprised me a little. I sure was thirsty."

"Was that the highlight of twelve days of running?"

"No, seeing you, Crystal, and the girls was," I said. Aaron flashed a quick smile and got his eyes back on the road.

As we drove up the six-mile grade to Crossville, I was still thinking about Crab Orchard and the mine and the snakes. What

143

I was *really* thinking about, though, was the truck that was pulled up to the loading dock that day that I thought maybe I recognized. I guess that now that I wasn't pounding the pavement eighteen miles a day; wasn't consumed with the many little distractions those eighteen miles created every day, blisters, hydration, food, rest, dodging traffic, and the big one – vertigo; now that those things didn't dominate my thinking, it was only natural that my attention would lean towards the truck driver mystery. I looked back over my shoulder. The big mountain behind the mine was still there. I was wondering if that same truck would return to that loading dock tomorrow – the first day of the new work week. Was that truck really the same truck that was at the Bar B Q joint? What were the odds? So what if it was?

Then it hit me. The same day of my spotting the truck at the BAR B Q joint, the same day I read the words on the truck's door – JETS – Jesus Express Truckers – Jabez, it was later that night I had the dream – the dream about that same truck, about the driver singing a trucker song. I even remembered the title, *Open Highway*. Okay, so what? That was all in a dream, right? Right. But here's the kicker. The voice of Jabez, the trucker in the dream, his Appalachian accent was identical, matched up perfectly, was one in the same as the voice that belonged to the real-life person who belonged to the 423-562-.... partial phone number, the one I couldn't remember all of it. Was I doing it again? Something I thought maybe I had done before – taking something from the real world and inserting it into my own dream world. Only this time I was doing it the other way around.

Then the kicker of all kickers floated through what remained of my sixty-eight- year- old lucidity and reasoning – the truck driver that Margie Babb gave her son's mittens to. Did he not match up with the other three: one in the dreams, another at the Bar B Q joint, and the voice of the phone number?

I was hoping that Aaron wasn't picking up on my growing frustration. I didn't think he was. I grabbed my cell phone and dialed 423-777-7777.

The Englishman answered, "Beyond Time, Before Creation." This time there was no "May I help you?" He continued, "Coach Finn, it's so good to hear from you. Everyone here wants to congratulate you on the completion of your run. You've been a wonderful, let us say, "Ambassador", for all of us here at the home office. And yes, we know why you are calling. You're interested in tracking down, maybe putting a positive I.D. on a trucker named Jabez who you believe may be associated with a partial phone number starting with 423-562-.... I've discussed this with the Boss, and I believe we'll have a complete number for you very soon."

I could hear static and timeless rumblings from far off galaxies and black holes. Then I heard what sounded like polar ice shelves shifting and screeching and wailing and lightning bolts from undisclosed planets. More static and crackle and then the Englishman was back. "It's getting quite busy and the weather has betrayed us. Call again soon, and just maybe, Coach Finn, there will be a new assignment." He was lost in the mayhem of colliding worlds, existences, dreams, reality, and Holiness.

"But wait," I said, "A new assignment?" There was no answer of course. I just sat there watching Tennessee slide by, outside the window.

"Dad, who were you talking to?" Aaron asked.

"I'm not sure. No, I don't know."

"Dad. Are you okay?"

I figured I was okay enough, but I was wondering if I had a new assignment.

CHAPTER 18

The sun had descended behind the hills just west of my house when we pulled in the driveway. My neighbor, Buff, had left a note taped to the backdoor. It said that Oscar and Shirley had been fed around noon and that was also the last time they'd been out of the house. When I unlocked and opened the door, Oscar was all over me. He wanted me to run with him, but I sent him off solo. Aaron came in to use the bathroom, grab a snack, and fix us some coffee. He wasn't staying. In a half hour he was driving back east.

I checked my phone for text or voice mail asking about Christian counselling. I remembered that I had put a message on, saying I wouldn't take calls for two weeks, but there were still close to twenty voice mails for me. I had just let them stack up. It was Sunday, of course, and I knew the Good Book said it is a day of rest, but I wasn't tired. I said a quick prayer asking the Lord to forgive me and then I answered several calls.

The first call was from a teenage boy who said his stepfather would not allow him to be baptized. The boy was sixteen, his mother had died from a fentanyl OD, and Bob, the stepfather, was still heavy into drugs. The boy also said the stepfather was a truck driver, but I didn't place any particular significance on that. As things turned out, that fact would become important. I asked the boy why Bob wouldn't allow him to be baptized.

"We don't go to church or anything. He doesn't want me being around kids that do, or read the Bible, or anything like that."

"I see," I said. The boy's name was Nate. I said, "Nate, I believe you're plenty old enough to make your own decisions on things like this – spiritual things." I was thinking about what Bob might do if Nate attempted a secret baptism on his own at some local church. I knew however, most preachers would avoid any such thing.

"Nate, try to tell me why you want to be baptized."

"I'm not sure. I've been thinking about the God thing, you know, who He is, what He's like. I don't know anything about Him. There's these kids at school that say you got to be baptized before you can learn stuff about God."

"I'm not sure I agree with that, Nate. Look, here's what I would suggest you do: Do you pray, Nate?"

"I sort of try sometimes. I'm not sure how you really do it, or if God hears you." He sounded pretty lost.

"Oh, He hears you, Nate. Look, when you pray, Nate, it's like you're talking to your best friend, it's like …" I realized that trying to describe sincere prayer was not nearly as good as demonstrating it. "Nate, let's you and me pray together, okay? I'll help you if you get stuck. Does that sound okay?"

"I guess so."

"Good. Close your eyes, Nate. I'll close mine. Hello God. Nate and I are going to talk with you for a few minutes. We thank You, Father God. We thank you for loving us and being our very best friend. We thank You for Your Son Jesus. And we know, He loves us too, God. I'm asking You to please hear every word that Nate prays. Nate and I thank You for doing it. We know that You will. And God, we ask You to guide Nate in everything he does and we know that You will. Father God, please teach Nate what baptism means and when he's ready, we'll get him baptized.

"Okay, Nate, it's your turn."

"Uh, …" Thirty seconds went by. Silence.

"It's okay, Nate. Just say hello to God, and see what happens."

"Okay. Hello God …" Another thirty seconds. Silence.

I broke the silence, "Nate, you still there?"

"Yeah, I'm here. You didn't hear him?"

"Hear who?"

"God. He, uh, He said hello back to me and He talked to me. I swear. I heard him."

"You heard Him talking to you?"

"Yes sir. I swear."

"What did He sound like Nate? What did He say?"

"He had, I guess you'd say, a country accent, you know, like He lives way up in the mountains or something. You don't believe me."

"I believe you." Oh boy! Did I believe him! "Go on, what did He say?"

"He said the same thing you said – that I was old enough to get baptized, and He said He loved me."

"Anything else?"

"He said you'd baptize me."

I was thinking, maybe, was this supposed to be my new assignment? I didn't know what to say to Nate. Was I qualified to baptize? If God said I'd do it, how could there be any wiggle room? There might have been some, but I couldn't see where it was.

"Okay Nate, we'd better get busy and get you baptized. You want to do it, right?"

"Yes sir."

"I agree. I think you need to be baptized and I'd be honored to do it. But Nate, let me tell you the truth. I've never baptized anyone before. I want to pray on it for a couple of days and then we'll do it. Is that alright with you?"

"Yes sir."

"Okay, call me back on Wednesday and we'll get you baptized."

"Yes sir, thank you."

I took several more voice mails from my phone and ended up with two appointments at their homes in the next few days. When I went to bed, I was satisfied that I'd done about all I could do for one day. I wasn't sure my new assignment would turn me into a modern-day John The Baptizer. I was only doing what I'd always done since my new existence started twenty days ago. I was following the signs.

Sunrise caught me in the kitchen making coffee and fighting off Oscar. Not today, old buddy. I put him outside and picked up Shirley to give her a little attention. She purred a little and then did what cats are so good at doing. She ignored me, jumped down, and trotted away.

I took my coffee with me to my desk, fired up the computer and studied everything I could find in the Bible about baptism. I had already known much more than I thought I knew. If you could condense everything I already knew and everything I learned that morning, I don't think you could do any better than twenty-six words Jesus spoke in Matthew 28:19: "Go therefore and make disciples of all the nations, baptizing them in the name of the Father and of the Son and of the Holy Spirit." Add to that, I understood the symbolism water played in the ritual. You want to wash away the sin and corruption of the old. You want to present yourself before God with a clean spirit. I felt like I was prepared to baptize young Nate. I looked forward to Wednesday when I expected him to call back.

The next thing on my "to do" list was catch up with Renae Holsclaw. Today was the day she was supposed to have her sentencing hearing. Of course, that was before her fourth arrest about a week ago. When she answered the phone, I couldn't tell if she was happy or sad. "Coach Finn, I'm going to prison for a year, but it's okay, your friends the Barkleys are going to foster care my baby."

"They're going to foster care Wendy?"

"Yes sir. They said you gave them my number. They called me and said they wanted to take good care of Wendy until I get my freedom back and then, they said they would make sure, whatever it took, that I'd get her back. Coach Finn, I'm sorry."

"What do you mean?"

"I lied to you. I went to that party willingly. I probably used more drugs than anyone there. I'm so sorry."

"Renae, maybe God has worked this out for the best."

"I know I need to get straightened out, so when I come back, I can be a good mother."

"Sounds like a good plan. When are they taking you in?"

"Tomorrow morning. I waived my right to a trial on the fourth charge. The judge said that under the circumstances he saw no reason not to speed everything up. A new sentencing hearing was held Friday. He said this way will get me back to Wendy the quickest way possible."

"What do you think?"

"I think he's right."

So, it seemed like the first two cases in my Christian counselling career had somehow woven themselves together. And it seemed like they had much better results than you might have expected. Who knew what to expect? The last twelve days had proven that with God all things were possible. I was following the signs and holding on to the tail of the tiger. Holding on, yes, holding on, hanging on, clutching that unpredictable tail, not wanting to let go. And, you know what was strange? I wanted more. I wanted all I could get, all He would give me.

I remembered yesterday, Aaron and I driving back from Knoxville. The receptionist at 423-777-7777 had said: "Call again soon and just maybe, Coach Finn, there will be a new assignment". I started dialing.

"Beyond Time, Before Creation, may I help you?" The British accent was sharp and clear. There was no interference with the signal; no clamorous background reverberation I had heard on other calls.

"Good morning, sir. This is Finnegan Weaver. I called yesterday and was told I may be getting a new assignment. Also, I believe you said you would look into the mystery of the partial phone number. Truth be told, I have a third concern I was hoping you might address."

"Ah, yes, Coach Finn. I think I know what the third concern might be. Please confirm my suspicions, tell me what it is."

"It's your identity, good sir. Every time you say you will run something by the Boss, I get this feeling, sir, that maybe you are the boss and you are hiding behind the guise of the receptionist to muddy up the water as to your true identity."

His voice was about to adorn itself with the tone of insult, as if I had affronted him in some way. "Think what you are saying, Coach Weaver. You are accusing the Boss of being deceitful. You know good and well that God The Father has never, could not ever, would never deceive anyone."

I was knocked off my wiseacre, know it all pedestal. Knocked clean off. I knew he was right. But he wasn't through, not by a long shot.

"Do you ever read God's word, Coach Finn? What's the matter with you? Don't you remember Hebrew, chapter six, verse eighteen?

"So that by two unchangeable things in which it is impossible for God to lie, we who have taken refuge would have strong encouragement to take hold of the hope set before us.

"And this from The Psalms:

"You are near, O Lord, And all Your commandments are truth.

"Have you never read what Jesus, Himself, said?

"You are a king then? You say that I'm a king, Jesus replied. I was born for this and I have come into the world for this: to testify to the truth. Everyone who is of the truth listens to My voice."

I had to stop him. "Of course. I never should have said what I said. I'm sorry."

153

"You're sorry! Is that all you can say? You listen to me, Coach Finn. I will leave you with one last thought, and I suggest you let it sink in good. Then maybe, just maybe, we could start this conversation all over again. From The Revelation, we read:

"And He who sits on the throne said, "Behold, I am making all things new." And He said, "Write, for these words are faithful and true."

"Call me back in two hours."

Oh boy, I felt like my second- grade teacher had put me in the corner and all the kids were laughing at me. No, I felt much worse than that. How could I have accused God of deceit? I put my running shoes on and headed out the door. Oscar was sniffing around a tree over by the woods. I hollered over in his direction, "Come on, let's go."

We took off like a rabbit with a tail-end of hot buckshot. I ran as hard as I was capable of running until finally, I went down. It took Oscar twenty seconds to catch up to me. It wasn't the vertigo. It was my defeated spirit, my contrition. I rolled around in the weeds I had fallen in. I shed tears of remorse and penitence. After a while, I got up and dusted myself off and started walking back to the house. I took a shower, dressed, and went to my desk. I picked up my phone and dialed 423-777-7777.

"Two hours exactly," the British receptionist said. "I kept this line open just for you. It was my conjecture you'd be precisely punctual."

"I always try to be. It's like I always taught my ball players, a good back-door baseline pass to a cutting wing has to be on-target and on-time."

"Yes, but I don't believe you called back to discuss basketball."

"That's right. I didn't. Let me first ask that you understand why I said the foolish things I said two hours ago. I'm new at this level of spiritual adventure. Three weeks ago, I thought I was having a heart attack. Since then, I've run over two hundred and twenty miles and been involved in the most phenomenal, the most thrillingly charged spiritual events of my life. Frankly, I think I'm a little overcome with the shock of it all. I guess the final tipping point was my suggesting that Father God might be deceitful. I know how wrong that was. I'm so ashamed."

"All perfectly understandable," the receptionist said. "I've been in similar circumstances myself."

"Of course you have," I said. "You're human, aren't you? You're just like me."

"I'm not sure I'd go that far. We are all different. Each of us has a role to play."

"What I'm trying to say is, you are actually flesh and bone, right. You're not an angel, not a time traveler, not a modern-day Moses."

"I'm a receptionist. As far as flesh and bone … of course. But there's more. Just like you, there's more."

"What's your name?"

"Percival. Percival Whittington. My friends call me Percy."

"Okay if I call you that?"

"It is my wish that we consider each other friends. You've known all along we're on the same side."

"Of course I have. But now I'm not so much in the dark. I think I'm starting to put some of the pieces together. You really are a receptionist. You actually man a switchboard for folks who want to communicate with God."

"There are not as many of those kind of people as we'd like to see. The way it's worked out for me is I'm the link that the Father uses to get in touch with humans."

"Sure Percy, I can see that. But how come the first call I got from 423-777-7777 was not from you. It was from an old man from the Tennessee mountains. I remember the voice well. It wasn't yours. Plus, I've heard that voice several more times, even in some dreams."

"Yes, of course. Look at it this way. Do you think just one receptionist could handle all the traffic between God and mankind?"

"You're saying the man, the Appalachian voice, he's just like us. He's flesh and bone."

"Don't forget, there's always more than just flesh and bone." The signal was gone. The scrapes and grinds of the humongous cosmos called eternity returned. I sat there at my desk thinking it all through – laughing and chuckling a little – to myself of course, there was no one else to share it with. Oscar came to me and rubbed at my knees and then he looked up. He was giving me the dog equivalent of a laugh and a chuckle.

A few minutes later my phone gave me the signal that a text message had arrived: *Regret to inform you I will no longer be your link to Beyond Time, Before Creation. The Boss has assigned a new receptionist to your account. You will be receiving your new assignment soon. I have been honored to serve you. Your honesty, faith, and service has encouraged me, has elevated me, and reassured me that we who are always much more than mere flesh and bone, that is, all of God's children, will meet again when the Father brings us all home. Sincerely, your friend, Percy.*

CHAPTER 19

I spent the rest of the day catching up on the calls to my counselling service. Most of them I handled with good conversation and prayer. It amazed me to learn how many people get into a depressed state simply because they don't have anyone they can talk to. I felt like I was really helping people. I felt good about what I was doing. I also felt good about the words of praise Percy had left me with. Thinking about the way he signed off in his text message, I had a suspicion that maybe, somehow, I had gotten him in trouble with the Boss. After thinking about it, I discounted that theory. I looked at his reassignment to other cases as probably a promotion for Percy. I was wanting to think that my service to the Father was ordinary, nothing any serious Christian wouldn't do. Percy was probably more useful to the Boss by working on higher level cases.

The next morning I started my day thinking about how to arrange Nate's baptism. What about his stepfather? Should we hide it from him? I was trying to think it through. I didn't want to make any mistakes on something as important as baptism. My phone went off.

"Finn Weaver, may I help you?" I said.

"Yes sir. This is Nate."

"Good morning Nate. You're not in school today?"

"No, I didn't go. I was supposed to call you back tomorrow, but I couldn't wait. Bob's been all over me. I really want to get baptized."

"Is he there now?"

"No. Yes, I mean he's outside in his truck. I'm inside the truck stop."

"Spell it out for me, Nate. What's going on? I'll try to help, if I can."

"I was gonna' go to school today but Bob said no, you ain't going today. He said he didn't want me around those Christian kids. He said I'd be with him today. But I found out what he meant was, I wasn't *ever* going back to that school. He didn't know it, but I heard him on the phone last night. I think it was his dispatcher. I heard Bob tell him that we'd be in Denver in two days – me and Bob. When I got up this morning, all our clothes and stuff was gone from the apartment. He packed them into his truck. He's taking me with him to live in Denver."

"How do you feel about that?"

"I don't want to go."

"What's he doing outside in the truck. When are you leaving?"

"I guess an hour from now. A woman got in the truck and he told me to go inside and stay in the restaurant and he'd come in and get me in an hour."

I knew I could be getting into plenty of trouble if I acted on what I was thinking about doing, but I did it anyway. Maybe this was supposed to be my new assignment? No, I didn't think it was, but still, something had to be done about this sixteen-year-old who wanted to be baptized and was about to be hauled off to a new town he didn't want to go to. Notice, I didn't say kidnapped, or abducted. As Nate's stepfather, I'm sure Bob had legal status and that's why I was risking plenty of trouble.

"Nate, what truck stop are you at?"

"The Pilot."

"Nate, sit tight. I'll be over there in twenty minutes. I'll figure something out; maybe you won't have to go to Denver. What kind of clothes are you wearing?"

"A green hoody and I got a white hat."

"Stay in the restaurant. I'll find you."

As soon as I got in my car, I called the Montgomery County Sheriff's Department and asked to speak to Wilson Nesbitt, my friend who also happened to be the Sheriff. The receptionist said please wait, Coach Finnegan, I'll see if he's available.

It didn't take twenty seconds. "How you doing Finn? What can I do for you?"

"Wilson, I want to ask a huge favor. I've got a possible situation developing."

"Talk to me. I'll do what I can."

"Wilson, I've got a sixteen-year-old boy who may be kidnapped in the next hour. He's safe right now, but things could go south. Look, I think if you could get me a patrol car over here, I think just that show of force could save us all a lot of real trouble. I think we can nip the whole thing in the bud with a police presence of an officer in a cruiser. If things go bad, there's going to be an arrest, a night judge, human services, and other problems. Give me one of your men for twenty minutes. I think we can avoid all that unnecessary disturbance."

"Coach, if this was anybody else, I'd say forget it. Where do you want the cruiser?"

"The Pilot truck stop. Have him wait for me. I'm on my way. Don't worry, Sheriff. This will not be a heavy scene."

Famous last words come in many forms. "Hey y'all, watch this," comes to mind. "No problem, I'll take care of it," is another one. "Don't worry Sheriff," was one I was hoping wouldn't lead to disaster.

I drove as fast as I dared. I swept around the city on the southern by-pass and floored it when I got on the interstate. In ten minutes, I was pulling into the truck stop. The big, modern truck stops aren't just truck stops anymore. They've become "travel centers". In many ways they remind me of Greyhound Bus Stations. In fact, many of them serve as rest stops for the Greyhound transit lanes. The difference is the travel centers cater to a much more diverse travelling public. All socio-economic classes are represented, not just the tired and lowly masses who can't afford anything else.

The Pilot, just north of Clarksville had twenty automobile fuel pumps out front and parking for fifty or more units. Around back there were another twenty fuel pumps for the trucks. These were diesel pumps and it took all of eight minutes for a pump to fill a truck's twin one-hundred-gallon tanks. There were ninety-five parking spaces for the 72-foot tractor trailers. That space gobbled up four acres.

I saw a Montgomery County Sheriff's patrol cruiser parked quietly down on the end of the main building where the restaurants, gift shops, rest rooms, and check-out counters were. There was an empty spot next to the cruiser and I pulled in

162

there. The officer looked and saw I was getting out and walking around to his window. The window was open when I got there. I looked down and said, "Thanks for coming. I'm Finnegan Weaver. The Sheriff sent you, right?"

"Yes sir, Coach. I know who you are. What do you got going on? I got back-up a mile from here, if we need it."

"No, no. We're not going to need anything like that. Can I get in for a minute?"

"Sure." I heard the door lock click on the other side. I walked over and climbed in. I saw his name etched on a square plate pinned to his uniform – Corporal Ted Albright.

"Corporal, here's the deal. There's a sixteen-year-old boy inside. He's told me that a man, a truck driver, wants to yank him out of school here and take him to Denver with him. This is completely counter to the boy's wishes. The man is the boy's stepfather. I suppose that gives him legal authority to take the boy with him. But, Corporal, there's a dark side to the story, and we don't have enough time to go into it. The stepfather is outside in his truck. He sent the boy inside a half hour ago when he invited a woman into the truck with him. He told Nate, the boy, he'd come in to get him in one hour. Now what I want to do is spend a few minutes with the boy, then I want to go out there and talk to the stepfather. I believe with your help I can get him to change his plans of forcing the boy to move to Denver with him."

"Coach, I see all kinds of problems here, but the Sheriff sent me to assist you. What do you want me to do?"

"Good. I'm going in to talk to the boy. I won't be long. When I come out, I am going to walk all the way around to the back, find the truck, get in and talk to the man. If I'm successful, we'll all go home happy, and the boy won't be drug

163

off to another state. If I'm not successful, well, I guess we can say that we tried. Corporal, what I want you to do is drive back there and just hover around. No flashing lights, no siren, just be back there moving around so he can see you. Okay?"

"No problem. Then what?"

"If I don't climb down out of the truck in ten minutes, I want you to pull up close with your lights flashing. Don't block him in, just get close and keep the lights flashing. From right then, something, one way or another should happen in the next five minutes. Okay? I don't expect any kind of trouble. We'd just be putting a little persuasion on him, that's all."

I left the cruiser and walked in the truck stop. There were four or five people lined up at the check-out, at least twenty in the two fast food outlets, another ten were shopping the retail area, and finally a steady stream of truck drivers was moving around down by the diesel check-out desk. Although it was busy, the store looked like it could hold a lot more traffic.

I headed for the fast-food restaurants and spotted Nate easily. He had the green hoody and the white ball cap. He was sitting at a booth by himself, and it looked like he'd about finished an order of fries and a coke.

I walked over and sat across from him. "Hi Nate, I'm Finn Weaver." He looked shy. He wasn't a big kid, but he looked like he was thoughtful and that he could take care of himself.

"Yes sir, I'm glad you came. Are we going to do the baptism?"

"You still want to?"

"Yes sir, more than ever."

"Good. Yes, we'll do it right here. Then I'm going out and talk to your stepfather."

"You won't change his mind about anything."

"Maybe not. But at least he'll have an opportunity. Now, are you ready to be baptized?"

"Yes sir."

"Nate, this is a special time in your life, a holy time. This is a day you'll never forget. I'd like you to read this." I handed him a one page print out. In it was the basic information describing the Methodist sacrament of Baptism. He read it and then I said, "You good with everything?"

"I think so."

"Brothers and sisters in Christ: Through the Sacrament of Baptism, we are initiated into Christ's holy church. We are incorporated into God's mighty acts of salvation and given new birth through water and the Spirit. All this is God's gift, offered to us without price.

"Nate, do you renounce the spiritual forces of wickedness, reject the evil powers of this world, and repent of your sin? Say 'I do', Nate, if you agree to this."

"I do."

"Nate, do you accept the freedom and power God gives you to resist evil, injustice, and oppression in whatever forms they present themselves?"

"I do."

"Nate, do you confess Jesus Christ as your Savior, put your whole trust in his grace and promise to serve him as your Lord, in union with the church which Christ has opened to people of all ages, nations, and races?"

"I do."

"All praise to you, Eternal Father, through your Son Jesus Christ, Who with you and the Holy Spirit lives and reigns forever. Amen."

I grabbed the small vile of water I had in my pocket, and as I leaned across the table and sprinkled it on Nates head, I said, "Nate, I baptize you in the name of the Father, and of the Son, and of the Holy Spirit."

He looked up at me and his eyes were quietly vibrating the question *Am I baptized now?* I said, "Yes, Nate, you are a new person, a new spirit." I followed that with, "Through baptism you are incorporated by the Holy Spirit into God's new creation and made to share in Christ's royal priesthood. We are all one in Christ Jesus. With joy and thanksgiving, I welcome you as a member of the family of Christ."

Nate wasn't sure it was over or what to do. I stood and motioned him to do the same. I put a big hug on him and gave him the gift I had brought with me – a new Bible.

"Thank you for baptizing me and for the Bible. Bob's not going to like it."

"You wait here, Nate. I'm going to talk to him. What's his truck look like?"

"It's red, dirty, number 842 on the door, parked on the second row."

"Okay. Don't worry. I'll be back." There were those words again – don't worry.

I went out the front door and noticed that Corporal Albright was backing out slowly. I walked past him and then around the end of the building and then back in the parking area of the big 72-foot, 80,000-pound tractor trailers. I spotted a red truck on the second row. It had 842 on the door and Nate was right, it was covered up in road grime. As I walked towards the truck it occurred to me that I might want to record whatever was about to happen. I turned on the video recorder on my cell phone and was able to get it wedged into my shirt pocket with a handkerchief in such a way that the lens was unobstructed. In effect, it became a body cam.

I was approaching the truck from the passenger-door side and as I got within thirty feet, l saw the door open and a woman stepping down from the two safety steps. When she became grounded, she slammed the door shut and turned to walk away. I cut her path off.

"Hey baby, you giving it away, or am I going to have to pay for a date?" I tried to make the pitch sound convincing, but I doubted whether I had succeeded. She looked quite ordinary, about average height, maybe just a little overweight. No make-up or jewelry. Her dress was a plain washed-out flower print and maybe three inches above knee length. Other than the dress, she looked as if she might have been a warehouse worker just getting off the graveyard shift.

"You a cop?"

"Ain't no way. I'm just a horny truck driver."

"Where's your truck?"

"Down at the end."

"Fifty bucks for a half hour."

"Okay, that's all I wanted to hear." I paused to let that sink in. "I'm not really looking for a date. What I want you to do is tell me how it went in there." I looked up at Bob's truck.

"What are you, a pervert or something? I ain't telling you nothin' about what I do in trucks."

"Oh, I sure hope you do this time. I'd hate to get the Sheriff down here." I looked back over my shoulder where Corporal Albright had his cruiser sitting quietly about fifty yards away.

"A cop. I shoulda' known it." She had venom in her teeth that I'm sure she would have sunk into my neck if Corporal Albright's cruiser wasn't down there.

"Look darlin', I'm not a cop. It's the guy right there." I looked back up at Bob's cab. "He and I have an issue. Let's call it a little family matter. I just want to know a couple of things about him. You'll be out of here in two minutes. Forget the Sheriff down there. I got him. You reading me here?"

"You'll keep the sheriff off me?"

"Yes Ma'am. I promise."

"Well, okay. He was rough, real rough. He hurt me. Not only that, he wanted to do a three-way with a young boy. I said no. He put the boy out of the truck and then he got mean with me. Real mean."

"Thank you. Get on out of here. Get home. Take this with you and give me a call tomorrow. You want to get out of being treated mean, rough, and dirty … you give me a call." I gave her one of my Christian counselling business cards and she walked away.

I looked up at the dirty, red, number 842 truck and realized that Bob had probably seen me talking to the woman the whole time; I could see him up there behind the windshield looking right back at me. I walked over to the driver's side door and was looking up at the window. I saw it sliding down. He rested his elbow on the sill and I could see his face inside, dark and cloudy from shadows inside the cab. "Hey Bob. I'd like to talk to you. Can I get in there with you?"

"You got no business with me, mister."

"Well, if that's the way you feel about it, I guess I'll just take this video I got of me and the woman talking … I'll just take it down there to the Sheriff." I looked down where Corporal Albright's cruiser was sitting. Then I decided to turn the screws a little tighter. I motioned for Corporal Albright to "come on down." I had a little chuckle to myself. The cruiser arrived in seconds; Albright stopped right in front of truck number 842. I went to Albright and asked him to hold right there where he was – my business with 842 wouldn't take long now.

I went around Bob's truck to the passenger side door, opened it and climbed up inside and dropped down on the "shotgun seat." Bob did not seem very happy to have an uninvited visitor inside his cab. I'm pretty sure he had equal disdain for Corporal Albright and his cruiser. I looked around inside the cab. Naked centerfolds were taped to the walls. The lower bed was a trash pit and it looked like the upper berth was just as bad. I looked at Bob and was shaking my head. "Do you really think this is a suitable environment for a young boy?"

"I'm taking him to Denver. We'll have a nice apartment there."

"Nice like this, huh?"

"It's none of your business."

I was looking back in the sleeper and saw something I missed the first time. "Whose blood is that. The woman's or did you smack Nate around a little bit."

"Cut myself shaving."

"It doesn't look to me like you've seen a razor in two weeks."

"None of your business."

"Okay, if you say so." I was quiet for a moment, then, "Just wondering … what kind of a sentence you reckon a man might get on a conviction of conspiracy to commit sexual assault on a minor?"

"You can't prove nothin'."

"I got the woman's words right here on this phone, not to mention whatever it was you did to her."

"What do you want?"

"Ah, words that tingle the senses. Look, don't make me go through this two or three times. If I run out of patience I'm going to climb down out of here and give my cell phone to the cop. You with me, Bob?"

"Go ahead, I'm listening."

"You'd better be." I pointed up towards the main building where Nate was inside, waiting. "When does Nate turn seventeen?"

"Another month."

"Okay, so that means that just a little more than a year from now, he'll be eighteen, a legal adult." Bob didn't say anything. "I have a plan, Bob. I think it could work out for you, I think it could work for me, and most importantly, I think it will work for Nate. You digging this, Bob? Look, I got enough right now to put you in jail. The problem with that is Nate would be off to Human Services and a state orphanage or a foster home. I don't want to see that happen. Bob, you could play ball with me on this and nobody goes to jail or human services. One year and a month, Bob. You leave him alone for one year and a month. Don't harass him about his Christian friends, or the baptism I just performed on him twenty minutes ago. Most of all, you don't touch him or hurt him in any way. That's the deal, Bob. That's all you have to do. Thirteen months from now I give you this phone. The evidence disappears." I stopped. He didn't say anything. "You don't go to jail. Thirteen months. You live halfway decent for thirteen months, you won't go to prison."

"You could download the stuff you got. You could get it out lots of ways."

"No, I couldn't, Bob. I'm a man of my word. I'm a Christian."

PART TWO

CHAPTER 1

What's next, Father God? I don't know how You did it. We got Nate baptized by playing the blackmail card. We got Bob to back off, I hope for at least thirteen months. There was no trouble, no violence. I felt maybe a little – tarnished (is that the right word?) – guilty (is that the right word?). How about licentious? Guilt was close enough. But I guess, Father God, there was no other way to get Bob to see the light. Huh, wouldn't that be something? If he *really did* see the light. It'll be interesting to check on things from time to time – see how it goes with Bob and Nate.

What's next? What do you have for me now? It started with counselling, led to road adventure, and now You have got me baptizing folks. What's next? Whatever it is, I'm ready. I don't need to be blinded on the road to Damascus, like Paul. Nope, I'm ready for more, just the way I am. I'm your servant, Lord, and I'm ready. What's next.

That's the way the twenty-third day of my new existence got started – a good solid talk with the Boss. It must have lasted ten minutes. After that, I laced up my running shoes and followed Oscar out the door. I roughhoused with him and then I said to him, "Okay boy, you lead the way. I'll follow." He took off heading for that four-mile loop down near the riverbanks. I was right behind him. Just like twenty-three days ago, we turned at the river and started the two miles back towards the house. And just like the last time, with about a quarter mile to go, I went down. It felt like there was a thick rubber band in my chest and it stretched, stretched, stretched until finally it snapped back with a thud that felt like a lumber jack sinking a broad ax into a Ponderosa Pine. This time I would not be getting to my feet and trotting merrily back to the house. This time, I was thinking, maybe I was down for the count. Oscar tried to get me to my feet, but there was nothing he could do.

I started another serious discussion with the Boss: Well, well, I had always told my wife Sarah, that when It was my time to go, I'd like it to be on a basketball court, playing hard, sweating like a fourteen-year-old on the first day of practice. Sure, she would say. Sure you would. Big stud athlete Finn Weaver dies on the court. Honey, I bet you and me both will end up like everyone else – old, cold, and lonely, dropping our head to one side, sitting in a wheelchair in an empty, bare hallway of a nursing home. Sarah was a wonderful human being. We had many good years together, thirty-five to be exact. But she surely could come up with some zingers. Plus, her sense of humor would sneak up on you. I joked with her one time by telling her that me and my assistant coaches had to fight off all the women when we were out of town on road trips. She said whatever kind of women might have been chasing us probably didn't have teeth or wear shoes.

It looked like I wasn't going to get my basketball court. I was flat on my back in the weeds next to my running trail. But at least I had been active. At least I had been doing something athletic – running. And that's all I ever wanted when my final reckoning announced its arrival- I just wanted to be moving, pushing my body, pumping it, bumping it, running it, testing it, getting the most out of it that I could. I imagine all athletic coaches feel the same. And to think, we got paid to teach the same thing to young people. I was thinking how blessed I was, the good health I had enjoyed for sixty-eight years, the career, my family, my teams. And on top of all of that, there was this miracle which I called my new existence. There wasn't a script writer in Hollywood that could have come close to what I'd been involved with the last twenty-three days.

I suppose I should have been content to let it all slip away, laying there in the weeds with my chest feeling like a popped balloon. The orderly thing to have done would have been to die. But I had never really gotten into orderliness or convention. I said, "Father, you know best. If You are going to take me home, you better do it right now, because if you don't, I'm going to get up out of these weeds and run. I'm going to run farther than Forest Gump ever dreamed of running. And that's what I set out to do.

It was three weeks later. I had rented my house to a family from my church that had been through some bad luck. The monthly rental I charged was about a quarter of the going rate. I was glad to help, plus the couple had agreed to dog-sit and cat-sit Oscar and Shirley. They had three kids. The oldest was a fourteen-year-old boy who ran cross country in the ninth grade. He and Oscar got along like fuzz on a peach.

Yep, it was three weeks after that second heart attack and I'd managed to run forty slow miles down the Natchez Trace Parkway. I'd been on the road for a week, which meant that I was only averaging about six miles a day. But hey, I wasn't on any set schedule. There was no place I had to be at any set time. I was enjoying the easy running and the camping out in the woods every night. The Natchez Trace Parkway is a beautiful, well maintained two-lane gem that runs through Tennessee, Alabama, and Mississippi. It's a national treasure which rivals any of the great non-commercial getaway drives. Think Blueridge Parkway and Skyline Drive – no commercial traffic, only a few tourists, lots of cyclist, and a few crazies like me – vagabonds, hikers, and ramblers. How different it was from running highway 70 from Nashville to Knoxville where there were plenty of restaurants and motels. Here on the Trace, I ate what I carried in my pack, and after seven days, my pack was empty.

The morning of the eighth day I made coffee, broke camp and started trotting off, still southbound, getting closer now to the Alabama state line, twenty-five miles away. I saw an exit-road off the Trace which hooked up to highway 64. I knew there would be some sort of a country store soon enough. I found it and went inside.

It was perfect. Not only did they have some of the essentials I needed – bread, peanut butter, sardines, granola, Gatorade and cheese – they also had a couple of tables you could sit down and enjoy biscuits and gravy, grits, and hot soup. Those items were self-serve, and I made sure I got plenty. There was one other person sitting at the only other table which was actually butted up against my table. She looked to be about forty-five or fifty. Her eyes were lively enough but they belied some sort of emotional pain back in there which she made no effort to conceal. She wore worn out slacks and a black jacket about two shades darker than her dry, rough skin.

"You sho' do eat like a man been out in da' woods fer awhile."

"Yes mam," I said.

"What'chu been doin', comin' down the Trace?"

"Yes Ma'am. I've been on it seven days. You're the first person I've talked to in seven days."

"You don't look like the kind of man that be runnin' from sumpin'. You must be runnin' t'wards sumpin'."

"I like the way you put it. Thank you." I noticed how thin she was and the way she kept watching me eat. "Ma'am, don't take this wrong. I see all you got is a cup of water. Could I get you something to eat? I mean, I haven't talked to another human being in a week. You seem like an awful nice person. Come on," I said. I got up to refill my plate and motioned her to join me.

She got up and was walking toward the hot food. A woman came out from behind the hot food area, "Lucille," she shouted, "I told you, you ain't getting' no more food in here."

I pulled a twenty out quickly and handed it to the woman. A minute later, Lucille and me were back at our tables.

"Thank you, mister."

"I'm sorry she yelled at you."

"It's okay. She done give me a lot of food I ain't neva' paid fo'."

"People are supposed to help each other out." I said.

"I reckon so. Ya' know, when I said you eat like a man dat' been out in da' woods, I was thinkin' 'bout my Russell. Sometimes he'd eat like a starved mule."

"Your husband?"

"Yes, suh."

"A starved mule that come in from the woods, right?" She laughed a little. She was eating her food slowly. I said, "Tell me about your Russell. You still got him?" I knew she didn't when I asked the question.

"No suh. He's in the prison, down in Louis'anna."

"Tell me what happened, Lucille."

"He had dogs, ya' know, fightin' dogs. His best dog, he called him Major Bill. That dog killed a white man's dog one night and the white man got drunk and come after Russell. They got into it real good. Russell killed that man, but it was self-defense, sho as I can draw a breath. My two cousins seen it, but they was four white men said they seen it too. Russell done been in Angola Prison Farm, hits been, eight years now."

"I'm sorry. When might he get out?"

"They give him life with no parole."

What could I say. Such a tragedy. It looked to me like the old south was alive and well. I talked with Lucille a little longer. I tried to give her some money, but she wouldn't take it. But I did get her last name and her address. Her last name was Burwell. When I finally left the store, I was in too much of a doleful sadness to start running. I just walked aimlessly down the road. Highway 64 was a primary state route and if I were to walk it all the way to Memphis, it would take nine or ten days. I spent that night in a motel in Waynesboro, Tennessee but the next morning's light had no answers to the blue funk I was in. I couldn't shake it. I felt miserable. I felt worse than miserable. I felt like the principles and ethics I'd been teaching for forty years had been jettisoned from human awareness.

I had coffee in the motel lobby and a piece of toast. I started walking again. I just couldn't gather any enthusiasm for running. Cars and trucks thundered by, no doubt on their way to work. I felt envious. They had a purpose. They had a place to go to. They had a job. What did I have? It had been over three weeks since the encounter with Nate and his stepfather, Bob, but still I had no new assignment. I didn't view the running everyday as an assignment. I had thought I would have heard from my new handler by now. Didn't Percy say I'd be hearing from him – a new receptionist I think he said. I was thinking about it and realized my phone had been dead for over a week. How would anyone have reached me when I was on the Natchez Trace with no outlet to recharge my phone?

The cars and trucks continued their busy and purposeful transitory activities. I was thinking I'd stop at the next little store I came to and charge my phone. Maybe there was something on it I needed to see. I picked up my walking pace and within a minute I opened it up into a lively jog. The jog advanced to an eight-minute-per-mile running pace. I was hauling you-know-what down the road. A big old tractor trailer blew by me too fast to read any of its markings, but not so fast I couldn't see that the tractor's paint job was solid red. And what was that I heard? Its airhorn? Indeed it was – seven quick unmistakable toots from its airhorn – seven.

It seemed like the air I was breathing began tingling with excitement, with hope. I remembered what Lucille had said, "You don't look like the kind of man that be runnin' from sumpin'. You must be runnin' t'wards sumpin'." Now I was running as hard as I could. My eyes missed the trees, fence lines, pastures, creeks, and houses off to the sides of the road. They were fixed straight ahead, a quarter mile; fixed on the top of the next hill. As I got closer, I could see the top of that hill levelling out and down maybe a hundred and fifty yards there was a big truck on my side that had pulled off. It sat back in there close to several trees with about half their fall leaves still left. The tractor was red and now I was getting close enough to read the markings on the door – JETS, Jesus Express Truckers and below that, the name, Jabez.

I walked up about five feet away. I could see the old man in there, behind the wheel. The window came down and he stuck his head out just a little, "I tried calling you, but I figured after a couple of days I better get out and see if I could find you." His deep Appalachian accent was unmistakable. What was this – about the fifth or sixth time I heard it?

I said, "How's my friend Percy doing?"

"You mean that English feller? He's a piece of work. You know, I never have figured out how the whole thing is put together. I mean the way our assignments are handed out and everything. I got some coffee I just brewed. Climb up in here and we'll jawbone on it a little bit."

I went to the other side, opened the door and climbed up inside. It was a lot different than the inside of Bob's truck. There were no girly centerfolds and everything was clean and in order. There was a wooden cross about a foot high pinned on a wall and a Bible was the only book I could see on a shelf.

By the time I got settled into the seat, Jabez handed me a cup of steaming coffee. I just sat there sort of like a fifth-grader in the principal's office.

Jabez started out with, "Percival Whittington, yes sir, a first-class specimen of some sort of spiritual being. Maybe a branch of The Holy Spirit; maybe an angel."

I said, "He told me he was human. I *think* that's what he said. I'm not really sure. When I pushed him on it, he said, 'There's always more than flesh and bone.'"

Jabez said, "That sounds like Percy."

"Tell me this, Mr. Jabez," I said, "The first two times I heard your voice on my phone, the number it was coming from was 423-777-7777. Then later, I was talking to you one day and you said your number was 423-562 and I never could get the rest of it. Something happened." I was confusing myself, so I shut up.

Jabez started again. "I get most of my instruction, my assignments, through dreams. I didn't know anything about Percy or the 423-777-7777 number until about three weeks ago. It was the day you confronted Nate's stepfather up in Clarksville. Don't ask me how I knew about that. I just did. Probably a dream. I've tried the 423-777-7777 number every day since then. It seems to be out of service. I'll tell you what I think. I think Percy really is some sort of switchboard operator. Some of your calls to me must have gone through his number. Was 423-777-7777 a feasible number? Must have been. Your calls got through to me, didn't they?"

I interrupted him. "I think that only happened two times."

"All I know is that my dreams have been telling me to head down towards Baton Rouge and that I would run into you and that you and me were going to be given a shared assignment." He stopped and began sipping his coffee. "You know," he said, "like our first shared assignment – the tattered mittens."

"I didn't do anything at all. The homeless man gave them to me."

"You know what I mean. You fed that man when he was hungry. You were part of the chain. The sweet grandmother was part of the chain. And yes, even me, an old timey mountain truck driver. I was part of the chain."

I looked at the older than dirt truck driver, "Did you say you were heading down towards Baton Rouge?"

"Those were my instructions."

"Isn't the Angola Prison Farm near Baton Rouge?"

Jabez was quick with his reply, "it's about forty-five miles north of Baton Rouge. Matter of fact, the load I got in my trailer is going to the Angola Prison."

"You're kidding," I said.

"Do I look like a kidder to you?"

CHAPTER 2

"How are we supposed to do it?" I asked.

"I thought you'd be telling me that. All I know is I was supposed to find you and then get this load down to Angola."

"I guess I better tell you about the woman I met yesterday." I told him everything Lucille told me.

"Whoooeee! I've never tried to break a man out of prison, especially a place like Angola."

"That's it, huh? We're supposed to get him out of there?"

"You tell me," Jabez said and poured us both more coffee.

"Oh yeah. That's what it looks like. I've been a wreck since I talked to Lucille."

"Well, like we say up in East Tennessee, 'If you got somethin' to do, you best get ta' doin' it.'"

The truck had been idling the whole time we were sitting there. Jabez pushed in the two air brake release valves on the dash and I heard the hissing and felt the truck wobble a little. We were rolling and Jabez worked through ten gear-shifts to get the rig up to highway speed. We were going to Angola, Louisiana, to break a man out of, arguably, one of the toughest prisons in the United States. It had a long, sordid history of brutal, malicious, and merciless treatment of inmates whom eighty percent of them had been sentenced to life without parole for murder, rape, and worse. To be fair, it was the inmates themselves who were responsible for a good deal of the harsh conditions at Angola. Every story you've ever heard about inhumanity and prisoner on prisoner violence, occurs at places like Angola, every day.

The drive down to Angola took about six hours. Some of the time I used to attempt to figure out exactly who Jabez was. Talk about trying to get blood out of a turnip. But he did tell me a little about the JETS. It seems that he, and another trucker named Toby Etheridge, formed the group up about fifteen years ago. The reason they existed was to do God's will while driving the highways and byways all across America. In that aim , they had been involved in some incredibly extraordinary and memorable spiritual battles with the forces of darkness. Some of the tales he spun left me scratching my head and wondering how these things were possible. Then I realized I was riding along with him on our way to break a man out of Angola – a man neither one of us knew.

By the time we got close we succumbed to the realization that nobody was going to be broken out of Angola with six hours of planning. We were thinking, just possibly, we could pull it off in the next three months. We talked and talked and talked about different scenarios as to how we might get Russell Burwell out. What we came up with was, that in order to get him out, we'd have to get me in. No, I was not going to concoct some fake monstrous crime hoping that the outcome would reward me with a lengthy and just sentence to the infamous Angola State Prison Farm. I had a much more devious and deceitful scheme. I ran it by Jabez. He agreed, it was the best shot we had.

The closest town to the prison was Laurel Hill. That's where Jabez dropped me off around 7 PM. I checked into a motel and began formulating detailed plans as to how I might be able to deceive the warden into thinking I had a good reason for wanting to become part of the prison staff. Jabez, on the other hand, drove on out the nine miles to the prison. It was normal operating procedure for truckers delivering loads to park outside the main gate the night before the 10 AM delivery appointments were implemented. And, of course, the last thing we wanted to do at this stage of our plan, or at any stage, was to reveal any kind of relationship between Jabez and me. Jabez, in fact, would have no part in the escape plot until the day we actually sprung Russell Burwell. That was not going to happen, if it happened at all, until at least three months.

The next morning, I was up at 5:30 googling up as much information as I could gather on Angola Prison. Anything I could find, I read, and made notes. My main interests were any recreational or athletic programs run for the benefit of the prisoners. Bingo! I learned that depending on who the warden was, Angola has had athletic teams in baseball, softball, touch football, and basketball. They also had a prison rodeo that garnered a good deal of attention. Every warden has been different. Some wardens had supported inter-prison leagues where a few games each year were played. Some wardens never allowed such activities.

By the time I worked up the nerve to call the current warden, I felt like the plan to spring Russell Burwell actually had a pretty good chance of succeeding, that is if, and this was a huge if – if I could sell the warden on the lies I was about to tell him. It was 9:45. I dialed the prison's main switchboard that was listed on their website.

"Good morning, Angola Prison. State your business please." The voice was male, no nonsense, but still, accommodating.

"Yes, good morning," I responded with the best crisp and official tone I could manufacture. "This is Finnegan Weaver, head basketball coach, Austin Peay Stat University." That was the first lie. I hadn't been a head coach in six years. "I'd like to speak to Warden Colfield."

"What did you say your name was?"

"Finnegan Weaver."

"Hold the line, please."

It was at least three minutes, then, "What is your call in regard to?"

"Yes, of course. I was with Governor LeBlanc yesterday. He suggested I call on the warden. It pertains to a prison program the governor is interested in." The lies were really stacking up now.

"What kind of a program?"

"Look, if you prefer, I can have the Governor call the Warden direct to confirm my credentials. Your name, sir? You know, in case the Governor ask."

"Hold the line."

It only took about fifteen seconds. "This is Sonny Colfield. Who is this? And before you run a line of crap by me, the Governor saw no one yesterday. He's ill. He's been flat on his back, for two days."

"Warden, I apologize. I had to use something to get by your gatekeeper. My name is Finnegan Weaver. I really am the retired head Basketball coach at Austin Peay up in Clarksville, Tennessee. That's all legit. You could check it out easily. I'm calling to schedule a face-to-face meeting with you. All I want Warden is ten minutes of your time. You'll either like my proposal, or you won't. Just ten minutes, Warden. What do you say?"

"Tomorrow morning – 9:30. Come to the main gate. The guards will escort you in."

"Thank you, Warden. I'll see you then." Oh boy. I was getting in. The question was, could I stay in?

The rest of the day I spent buying a car and buying some clothes. I ended up with a six-year-old Honda Accord and as for the clothes, I went with tan slacks and a couple of blue, button down, oxford dress shirts. After that, I still had most of the afternoon to walk around town and talk to as many people as I could. I guessed that Laurel Hill went around twelve thousand in population, and I was thinking that a good percentage of the citizens would have ties to the prison. I wasn't disappointed. Many had relatives, neighbors, or friends that either worked there currently, or had worked there in the past. Some of the people I talked to had moved to Laurel Hill to be close to their loved one – some unfortunate convict who slaved away every day in the broiling sun in Angola's notorious row-crop prison industry. The information I was collecting would prove to be critical in the meeting I had set up with Sonny Colfield.

That night in the motel seemed to drag on and on. I rehearsed at least twenty times the story I intended to slide by the Warden. Jabez called me around ten o'clock. He was a hundred and twenty miles west of Baton Rouge where tomorrow morning, he would pick up a load bound for Dallas.

187

We both agreed it was best not to make contact until it was time to spring Russell Burwell.

Trying to sleep was a failure. I went down to the motel pool and swam until my muscles screamed. My next attempt to sleep was successful. A hurricane off the gulf wouldn't have woken me up.

CHAPTER 3

I was up at six, showered, dressed, and in the motel lobby having breakfast by six forty-five. I went back to my room and rehearsed my fabricated script several more times and then fell to my knees in prayer: "Our Father who art in heaven, Hallowed be thy name. Thy kingdom come, Thy will be done, on Earth as it is in heaven. Give us this day our daily bread and forgive us our trespasses, as we forgive those who trespass against us. And lead us not into temptation, but deliver us from evil. For Thine is the kingdom, and the power, and the glory, for ever. Amen." I wasn't done. "Father, thank You for this day. I pray, Father, you give me the strength to do Your will today. I pray, Father, that what I am about to do today is what You'd have me do. I pray, Father, for Russell Burwell and his wife Lucille. I pray for every prisoner anywhere on this Earth that is locked up behind bars. I pray they will open their hearts to Jesus and ask Him to take control. They may be in prisons and jails, Lord, but they can be free on the inside, through Your grace, Your love, and Your mercy. Thank You again, Father, for all You do. Be with me in everything I do. I do it for You. In Jesus name I pray. Amen."

At 8:30 I climbed in the Honda and took the road aiming west towards the prison. There was some traffic going that way, but not much. I assumed that the change from night shift to day shift happened at least an hour ago. The drive out revealed mostly pastures, creeks, and low woodlands. It didn't look like urban sprawl was coming anytime soon. The closer I got to the prison, the farther the distance became between small, mostly unkept, country houses. From the maps I had googled, I knew that the "Big Muddy", the Mississippi River, provided the final security measure on three sides of the 18,000 acres of prison real estate. The only accessible land bridge was the direction I was driving in from – the east.

I was driving slowly all the way out, collecting my thoughts, making last minute adjustments to the story I wanted to use to deceive the Warden. At 9:15 it was show time. The main gate was a hundred yards in front of me. I parked in a small gravel lot off to the left and walked up to the guard shack on the right. Another guard shack flanked the entrance road on the left. High mesh fencing extended out and away from the guard shacks until it disappeared into a wood line. Inside, it looked like a more substantial security fence was topped with razor wire. An armed thirty-foot-high guard tower loomed just right of the lower guard shack I was approaching. The door to the guard shack opened and a uniformed guard said, "Come in."

"I'm Finnegan Weaver, to see Warden Colfield at 9:30."

"Yes sir. Empty all your pockets and give us your driver's license." There were two other guards in the room and all three leered at me as if I were a rare species of monkey that had just been discovered. I dumped what little I had in my pockets on a table and a guard placed it all in a manilla envelope and I noticed he scribbled something on it with a black marker.

"Against the wall sir. Spread your legs, please." He frisked me thoroughly and the next thing he said was, "The Warden will see you shortly. You're early. Sign this log for me." After I signed it, he said, "You can sit over there."

I sat down and they continued their visual scan as if I were a lab specimen under a microscope. One of the guards moved a little closer and said, "So you're the big-time basketball coach. I played back in the seventh grade, but then I flunked outa' school." His eyes were rolling and he had a slight grin.

"That'll do Robicheau," one of the other guards said.

"I's just talking with the coach. Ain't no harm."

Nobody said anything. All three of them found something to do – answering the phone, checking on traffic coming through the gate, but mostly they all monitored several video security screens.

It got to be 9:45, a phone rang, I heard a guard say, "Copy that." He came my way and said, "The warden will see you now." I followed him out of the guard shack and we piled in a prison security van. It took about three minutes to drive back in towards the different "camps" – clusters of cell blocks where prisoners were stacked like cord wood. On the way I saw hundreds of prisoners laboring in the fields. They were under the watchful eyes of mule mounted "bulls" – guards with sidearms and 12- gauge riot guns slanted across their saddle horns.

We arrived at a large parking lot which was nearly full of employee's cars and trucks and plenty of prison vehicles as well. More gates, more razor wire fencing to go through and an electronic card reader the guard used to open the door. The lobby was dry wall on three sides and cinder block in dull light gray with an opening that led back through a large hallway. There were two desks and some decent looking chairs in a corner. An old coffee table was there also. Several magazines were stacked neatly and a sign on the wall said "no smoking". My escort whisked us past the two women at the desks, and we were heading down the hall. The warden's office was at the end and large stained and polished double oak doors opened in front of us. A uniformed guard came out and started down the hall behind us. My escort led me in and right up to the Warden's desk. The room was medium sized and had two walls with bookshelves. Behind the Warden's desk on a shelf were framed family shots and what looked like several Louisiana government bureaucrats. One I recognized as the Governor.

Sonny Colfield didn't stand up. In fact, he looked as if my appearance caught his attention by mistake. I guessed his age around fifty-five. His jawbone was thin, his forehead broad. Silver gray hair was slicked back on both sides leaving a shiny pink pate. He wore no glasses, His eyes, a greenish gray, seemed to shoot out slivers of pencil lead.

He said to my escort, "That'll do, son. Come back and get him in ten minutes."

"Yes sir, Warden." I heard the door shut behind me.

He motioned me to a chair close to his large desk. I sat down and he said, "I want you to know, Coach Weaver, I don't appreciate any kind of deceit from anybody. The only reason I let you in here is because I believe you are who you say you are. Austin Peay, I believe is right on the Kentucky-Tennessee state line and unless my memory fails me, Coach Weaver, Kentucky was neutral in the war."

"I believe that history would confirm, Warden, that as many Kentucky boys fell for The Confederacy as fell for the Union."

"That may be, Coach Weaver. You've got nine minutes left."

Drum roll, the curtain is going up, the rubber is about to meet the road, time to step out on stage, the performance is beginning. I thought to myself, *might as well start with a doozy, a real whopper.* "Warden, I've been studying your situation down here for quite some time. Everybody knew you had huge shoes to fill when Burl Cain retired in 2016. Warden Cain got lots of national attention with his emphasis on bringing Jesus to the jail. Most statistics I've read state that violence in Angola was reduced by over twenty percent. Remarkable. All a result of Christian programs introduced by Cain. Ever since then, folks have been asking what has Sonny Colfield done to enhance existing programs, or what new programs has he introduced at Angola?

"I know, I know. You've done your level best. But let's face it, we both know that tongues are wagging out there, screws are tightening up. some say your job security is on the line." I paused to assess his response. He was like a cold slab of Alaskan Tuna. His eyes told me nothing. "Warden, I've come today to offer my services to you. I have a program that will dwarf your annual prison rodeo. I think your rodeo is called "The Wildest Show In The South", right? I've been a fan for years, as well as many other Americans. I've read that it nets over a million dollars every year – money that's pumped back into inmate educational programs. Warden, what if I told you we could have a program right here inside Angola that would easily raise over fifty million dollars a year? Probably a lot more. You'll get all the credit, Warden. My part of it will be easy. It's the kind of thing I'm good at doing. I can stay way back out of the way. You'll be getting the spotlight. People will know that your foresight, your judgement, your experience is what made the difference when you ushered the program in. Why, you'll be a national hero. Prisons everywhere will want to do the same thing."

His eyes shot darts, "Fifty million dollars. Who the hell do you think you're playing with? You've got five minutes left. It better be good. I'm liable to press charges against you for conspiracy to enter a state penal institution under false pretense. I could add a couple other charges on top of that and provide witnesses. I don't think you know what thin ice you're on here, mister."

"Warden, I'm going to run through the program quickly. I can do it in five minutes. All I ask is you give it a fair hearing. If you don't think Angola would be interested, I'll walk out that door." I allowed a short pause. "Warden, the racial demographics in your prison is 83% black, 12% white, and 5% Latino or others. The racial demographics in the NBA, The National Basketball Association, is almost exactly the same. Warden, when I run the numbers, I come up with nearly 2,500 of the 6,300 total prisoner population in Angola are black men between the ages of eighteen and thirty-five. Warden, do you know what kind of a basketball team I could put together from such a base? I'm not saying I could win an NBA title. I probably couldn't. However, I certainly could put together the kind of talent that could compete with the best at any level-college or NBA.

I allowed another pause because it looked like I was beginning to see something stir back in there behind those bullet eyes of his.

"And Warden … compete is all we need. You see, I have friends throughout the NBA – coaches, owners, players, even the commissioner – I've known him for years. Warden, do you know what my recent discussions with these people have been?" Another pause. His eyes were moving around by now.

"They've been this: What if I had a team from a prison that was interested in putting on exhibition games with NBA teams? Not just any prison, but a team from one of the toughest prisons; say an Attica, a Folsom, a San Quentin, or maybe Leavenworth. How about a team from Louisiana - the infamous Angola State Prison Farm?"

"Do you know what all my friends said, Warden? They said, 'How long will it take you to get your team ready, Coach Weaver?' And, you know what? They are serious. The commissioner put his marketing staff on it, and within a week they produced a report that estimated a bare minimum of a hundred million in TV contracts which would be split 50/50 with the prison that gets on board first."

I looked at my watch and said, "I've only got a minute left. Here's the thing. My friends in the NBA have kept these discussions totally private and confidential. They don't want to leak anything until I can prove to them I can put together a prison team that would put on a good show, would compete, would capture the imagination of the country. That's why you haven't heard anything about it. They've given me three months and they're hoping I'll be successful. My ten minutes is up. You bring me in, we'll work out all the details, I'll get the team ready and then you'll become the legend of all prison reform in the entire history of the United States. If you're not interested, Warden, I guess I'll be making trips to Folsom and Leavenworth to talk with their wardens."

He was very still and quiet, but his eyes weren't. They were on the move. Back in there somewhere behind the optical nerve things were jumping around. Visions were emerging as if they were some primordial prophecy that flew in from that humongous cosmos called providence. Finally, he picked up the phone on his desk and I heard him say, "Tell the guard to give us another thirty minutes."

The Warden got up out of his chair and sauntered over to a window where he gazed out. He pointed to a building maybe a quarter mile away. "That's our gym, Coach Weaver. There are two regulation courts and bleachers, but I'm afraid the bleacher capacity is only about five hundred."

I got up and joined him and I said, "Not to worry, Warden. TV cameras don't require much space."

The Warden said, "What's in it for you? You haven't said anything about getting a piece of the pie."

"That's a good question. I'm not interested in any of the pie. Here's my story, Warden: I retired from coaching six years ago, and I lost my wife at the same time. I've pretty much been a slug since then, just slowly putting one foot in front of the other. I wasn't involved in anything meaningful. Recently I've changed my tune. I guess you might call it a spiritual awakening. I'm now looking at every opportunity I can find to help others. Somehow the Good Lord has opened my eyes to maybe I belong in prison ministry. I started reading and studying, and it didn't take long to stumble on what Burl Cain was able to accomplish here at Angola. Again, I don't know how He did it, but the Good Lord dropped the idea on me, the idea that an exhibition prison team could actually challenge the NBA. I had no idea how much money could be raised until I talked to my NBA friends." I shut up. I thought he was sold, but I wasn't sure.

"We'll have to do a background check on you, it's state law, and we'll have to put you in some security classes."

"No problem. No surprise there."

"Where are you staying?"

"I've got a motel room in Laurel Hill."

"We will need to get you into some of our staff living quarters inside the prison grounds."

I knew he was sold.

CHAPTER 4

Things moved quickly. My background check was back in three days, but there were still security classes that were required by state law. The Warden exempted me from the normal two-week training. Instead, he put me with his top security officer. I shadowed him for 72 hours. I read a couple hundred pages of material covering everything from prisoner rules and regulations, to psychotic criminal behavior. And there was also some required reading on how prison staff interacted with the civilian world, particularly the media.

The Warden called me into his office on the eighth day. By now, I was "Coach Finn" and it looked to me like the Warden was willing to do almost anything to allow me to succeed at developing his prison basketball team. I walked into his office, and we sat in two comfortable chairs over near the window that looked out over one of the prisoner outdoor recreation areas. The gym was visible in the background. "Coach Finn, it's time for a heart-to-heart talk." I gave him my best attentive gaze, dripping with anticipation.

"We've jumped the fences we had to jump to get you in here. You are now a full-time staff member of Angola. Nothing has changed with your NBA friends, right? They want to keep the development of our basketball team under wraps. Right?"

"Yes sir, absolutely."

"Okay. You'll be referred to as our, uh … recreational consultant. Makes sense, right? We won't be openly calling you our basketball coach. That all comes after the three months. Make sense?"

"Yes sir, sure does."

"Good. I'll be helping you in any way I can. Just let me know what you want, what you need to get things moving."

"Very good of you, Warden."

"Now, Coach Finn, I must let you in on a little secret." It looked like his eyes scrunched down to pencil size and that they were loading bullets into the chamber. I didn't say a word.

"I want to trust you, but … I hate to admit it, I sometimes get this feeling; it's a strange sensation that sneaks up on me every now and then. It's a perception, a feeling, you know? Maybe a vibe, maybe an awareness that you are really here for another reason than putting together a basketball team." His eyes looked as if they sought the answer to all creation. "Why am I getting such a nasty suspicion?"

I figured the worst thing to do was to make a grand denial, as if this were the greatest affront to my character that ever happened to me. I did just the opposite.

"I don't know what to say." I think that helped. The steel in his eyes softened.

He started again, "I might be wrong. I *better* be wrong. I just want to let you know this: If there *is* something you are up to, you will rue the day I find out. That's capital R, Capital U, capital E. Got it?"

"Warden, you've got nothing to worry about with me."

From then on, I was in the gym twelve hours a day. I was doing what any coach would have been doing – assessing the talent, grading every player that came in and played in pick-up games, or the nightly cell-block games that were unofficial but the closest thing to any kind of organized league. The other thing I was doing was searching for Russell Burwell. I was always asking the guards, "Who's that, what's his name?" I asked the ball players the same thing.

It took two weeks. There was a game in progress on one court and there were eight or ten other men down on the other court. They were just goofing around, shooting baskets and blowing the breeze.

The guards never questioned me asking all the men's names. They knew what I was there for. Well, they sort of knew. They knew as much as the Warden and I wanted them to know. Still, speculation was increasing. What was this ex-college basketball coach doing in the gym all the time? The prisoners knew something was up. So did everybody in the entire Angola complex. But it was going to be at least another week or two before I started selecting the players I wanted. Only the Warden and I knew where this ship was sailing. And of course, only I knew that the ship's ultimate home port would be the escape from Angola of Russell Burwell. I would have to be extremely careful how I managed my contact with and communications with him. The first of those contacts I was going to attempt in about two minutes.

I was looking at a guy shooting a few half-hearted jumpers from about 16 feet. I asked the guard nearest me, "What's that guy's name?"

"Uh, that's Burwell, cellblock Alpha, Delta Camp."

"Burwell got a first name?"

"Russell. Russell Burwell. Life with no parole. Second degree murder."

I didn't say anything about Burwell, but I did ask about two or three other men. Also, I said, "Does that bunch come in here a lot?"

The guard looked at a clipboard on the wall, "Yeah, all four of them show up every Tuesday."

I kept looking around the gym and asking the guards about other players. I surely did not want to place any special awareness or attention on Russell Burwell.

Burwell left the group he was with and walked over by a water fountain at the end of the gym. The closest guard was probably forty feet away. I drifted off in the same direction, making small talk to different ball players and guards on my way.

I got to the water fountain first. I bent over and took a long healthy slurp. I straightened up and stepped aside as Burwell came to the fountain. "Russell, don't look up at me. I've talked to Lucille. She told me about the night you killed that man; she said it was self-defense. Is that true?"

"Who are you?" he said, but he kept his head down, still drinking from the fountain.

"Russell, I can get you out of here, but I must know. Was it self -defense or willful murder?"

"Self-defense," he said and he raised up but avoided looking my way.

"Do you want out. I can do it and get you and Lucille to a safe place, where you could have a good life together."

"You know I do, man."

"You'll have to do everything I say. It'll take us a while, maybe three weeks. Maybe more. Not sure. Go back out on the court. If a guard asks you what we talked about, just say, basketball, nothing else. Got it?"

"Yeah, sure."

"Good. We'll talk more the next time." I walked all the way around the gym and when I got back to where I started, I noticed Russell and six or seven others in a pick-up game. It didn't look to me like the guards were paying any more attention to Russell than they were to anyone else in the gym.

Excellent, I was thinking. Initial contact completed successfully.

That night, in the small house I was quartered in, I compiled a list of what I thought were the forty best basketball players among the prisoner population in Angola prison. The next day I went to the Warden's office with my list.

The Warden looked over the list and said, "How many of these forty will you scrape down to the actual team?"

"Fifteen. That's a standard roster at any level – high school, college, or pro."

"What else?"

"I'd like to have an assistant coach. I've had my eye on Corporal Trigget."

"Bundy Trigget. He played some college ball, didn't he?"

"Yes, he did. I think he'd be a good choice to work with me. He pulls a shift in the gym, I think three nights a week. I was hoping you could assign him there full time."

"What else?"

"I'll need a team manager. I've got my eyes on a couple of guys."

"Let me know. Anything else?"

"Not a thing. I'll be pulling these forty out and talking with them, also whoever the team manager will be."

"Get to it coach."

"Yes sir."

By the time the next Tuesday night arrived, everybody in the prison knew who the forty were going to be, and although there was little importance attached to the selection of the team manager, everyone knew who it was – Russell Burwell.

That Tuesday night, the gym was cleared of everyone except the forty selectees, Corporal Bundy Trigget, Russell Burwell, and five on-duty prison guards. Oh yeah, and me.

I gathered everyone into a group and sat them down on the bleachers. Coach Trigget was standing next to me. Burwell was sitting with the forty and the guards were randomly spaced out behind me. They were very relaxed, not menacing in the ordinary way. The big mystery was about to be pried open – not the NBA connection of course, but enough that I could get things moving in the direction I wanted them to move.

I stepped up a couple of feet closer to the men. "It's good to see all of you here tonight. God bless you and I want to thank you for the interest you've shown in the mission we are about to pursue. I believe everyone at Angola has wondered what exactly is it that I am here for. Everyone knew that I was a coach and that with the Warden's approval we are putting together some kind of a team." I heard footsteps back behind me and saw that the warden had come in the gym. He stopped and was listening to my spiel.

"Tonight, I want to answer some of the questions everyone's had. Yes, we are going to have a prison basketball team. I will be your head coach. My name is Finnegan Weaver, and I had a good career as a college coach. Corporal Bundy Trigget will be my assistant coach. Fifteen of you will eventually become our working roster. If you don't find your name on the final fifteen, do not despair. We will need you just as much as we need the first fifteen. I'll be pushing all of you very hard. There will be injuries, there will be some that can't hack it, etc. Also, the first fifteen will be scrimmaging the other twenty-five on a regular basis. You will always have an opportunity to break into the first fifteen.

"So, that's the good news. You now know what we are and who we are. The bad news is we can't let out any information at this point as to who it is we will be playing, or any specific league, or locations. Within two months we'll have a much clearer picture on all of that."

I stopped, looked back at the Warden, and said, "Warden, do you wish to add anything?"

The Warden stepped up where I was. "You men have a great opportunity in front of you, but don't for a second think it affords you any different treatment from any other inmate in this institution. As a matter of fact, we'll be watching you closer. Don't make us wish we hadn't given you a high degree of trust. Do what the coaches and the guards tell you to do, keep your noses clean and we'll get this basketball team moving." The Warden moved back towards the door he'd come in.

I got the first practice moving, "I want twenty down on the far court. Five minutes of layups and five minutes of passing drills. Take them away Coach Trigget. The other twenty with me on the other court. If you work hard, we'll get a little scrimmaging in. Let's go!"

I must say, I was feeling quite the fraudulent scam artist – telling all these lies, setting up these forty men for a violent crash landing. The thing was, *I was getting into it.* The whole idea of building a real team out of raw material had become a part of me. The whole coaching psyche, the bonding, the trust relationship you build with the players. It was all coming back. It had been six years since I'd had it. I had it now. But I knew I could not allow that fact to interfere with the real reason I was here – breaking Russell Burwell out of here. As the two groups headed for the courts, I pulled Russell Burwell aside. "You still want out?"

"More now than ever."

"Okay, I've got a plan. I think we can pull it off. You'll have to be ready to go at all times, and you'll have to trust me. We must establish a pattern. You will be my gopher, my right-hand man. All the guards and the players too will see it as your normal function – you know - team manager. You'll take care of our equipment and uniforms. The main thing is we want people to see us together a lot. Corporal Trigget too. Especially Corporal Trigget. He's the key to getting you out of here, only he doesn't know it. The three of us together, always talking, always interacting; that's what is going to get you out of here. The night we make our move, it's only you and me getting out. Remember, Trigget doesn't know a thing. To him, you are just the team manager. Got it, so far."

"Yes sir."

"Good. I'll let you know more the closer we get. Now, get down there and help Trigget with those drills."

"I looked around. The guards had paid little attention to me and Burwell talking. Hopefully, in the next couple of weeks they would be paying no attention."

The next night, at our second team practice, I pulled Trigget aside. He was a big man, just about the same size and weight as Russell Burwell, six-six and around two forty. His black skin also had the same dull copper tint that Burwell's had. These physical similarities I had taken notice of when selecting my assistant coach. As you may be suspecting by now, they are the exact reason I chose him; not his background as a college ballplayer. Oh, I remember him as a college player; sure did. He lit up my Austin Peay Governors one night for thirty points, twelve rebounds, five assist, and three blocked shots. He had played for the Southwestern Louisianna "Rajun Cajuns". Now, after only one and a half practices with our prison team, I was sure that he had the skill to be a fine coach.

Trigget, Burwell, and myself were in the middle of the two courts. Scrimmage games were heating up. I looked at Trigget and said, "Well coach, how do you think they look?"

"Pretty rough. It's going to be awhile. I think, eventually, we might be pretty good. There's some talent, but playing team ball, though, it's going to take a while."

"I agree. We've got a ways to go, but still, I want to start designing offensive and defensive sets for these guys. Would you be up for some skull sessions after practice, say, uh, for about the next week?"

"Sure, coach Finn. I can do that. In your office here in the gym?"

"You know what? I'd rather get off the prison grounds. I'm here all day, either in my house or here in the gym. Why don't we go out to that little diner? You know the one, about three miles down the road from the front gate."

"Yeah, that'd be all right. I'll let my wife know I'll be a little later."

When practice was over, Trigget jumped in my car and we headed out towards the front gate. That first night the guards double checked our I.D.'s and the staff security sticker on my wind shield. They checked the floor in the back seat and had me pop open my trunk. After the first couple of nights, they waved us straight through the gate.

The pattern was being set. If I could keep the charade going, I was going to spring Burwell sooner than I might have guessed. Trigget was buying my hocus pocus all the way. Part of it might have been because I was starting to drop hints that once we had the team shaped up, that I was thinking about moving on. The team would be his; it would be Trigget's team.

About three or four days after we'd been leaving the prison grounds for our basketball planning sessions, I drove off the prison grounds by myself and made the hour drive to Baton Rouge. I was concerned that just maybe the Warden had the technical capability to eaves drop on my cell phone connections. I bought a new phone and immediately dialed up Jabez.

It was good to hear his Appalachian twang coming through, "Howdy young feller, how's it going down there. You still in the belly of the beast?"

"I'm in it up to my ears. Where are you today?"

"Up here in Yankee land, Pennsylvania."

"I think I'm ready to bust him out of here. You still willing to get involved?"

"Still willing to get involved? Listen here, young whipper snapper, I'm on God's team. I'm a JET, a Jesus Express Trucker. He put me on this assignment with you for a reason. I ain't about to start questioning His reason, now, or anytime."

"Just getting Burwell out of here only solves half the problem. I told him I could get him and his wife, Lucille, to a safe place where they could have a good life together."

"Look here, grasshopper, why do you think I was assigned to work this mission with you? I've already got a good safe place all lined up for the Burwells. Trust me, it's beautiful and nobody will ever find them there."

"Are you kidding me?"

"Do I sound like a kidder to you?"

CHAPTER 5

I had talked with Jabez two more times in the next week. All final preparations were now in place. We were ready to make our move. I recalled that Angola's history of escape attempts was disheartening. I could not find any definitive numbers, but most researchers agreed that in the one hundred plus years of the state actually operating the prison, there must have been upwards of five hundred various escape attempts. Of that number there were a handful of attempts that were possibly successful. Only two certain successes are known to have occurred. The majority of the rest were captured and returned to face the harshest punishment imaginable. Many times that consisted of up to ten years of solitary confinement. The escapees that weren't captured died ugly deaths in the river and swamps, or were gunned down by the guards, or nearly devoured by the vicious K-nine unit. I also recalled reading that in Louisiana a conviction of conspiracy to cause a riot, an insurrection, or a prison escape was a felony. It could lead to a twenty-year sentence in Angola. I thought, that could be me.

Too late now. All the pieces were in place. It was thirty-five days since I had arrived at Angola and we were going to spring Burwell. The day of the escape I was in the gym at 8:30 AM. For over a week I had been pulling six of my ball players at a time from their normal daytime work assignments. I got them in the gym and did individual skill work, usually shooting practice, free throw technique, ball handling, post play, etc. The Warden was accommodating in anything I had up my sleeve when it came to preparing the team.

That day he visited my six-man practice session. I had the guys working on "boxing out" for rebounds when the Warden pulled me over to the side of the court.

"Corporal Trigget tells me you're making progress. You still think it's going to take three months, or do you think you might be able to speed things up a bit?"

"Three months, Warden. That's what's it's looking like." I couldn't say, *No, Warden. I'm leaving here tonight and I'm taking Russell Burwell with me.* No, I couldn't have said that – the truth. The Warden hung around a little longer and I told him that when the time did come, there would be about eight NBA officials paying us a visit. "A big inter-squad scrimmage game will tell the tale, Warden. If they like what they see, they will be prepared right then and right there to sign a contract with you. They've told me you can expect a five-million-dollar binder check – a good faith demonstration to get things moving." That seemed to satisfy him. I heard him whistling as he walked away – "Sweet Georgia Brown", you know, the theme song for the Harlem Globetrotters.

I continued playing out my daily routine. I had another six-man practice session, and then I left the gym at 3:30. I drove the mile and a half over to the "B-line", the staff housing area. I

212

went in the house and made a sandwich, but I wasn't in the mood to eat. I sat down at my desk and was thinking everything through, rehearsing the scenes that would unfold later tonight. It was then that I realized I had a tremendous flaw in the whole scheme. I had plans for Russell Burwell; I had plans for Jabez – how his participation in the escape would be carried out. But I had no plans for myself – after the escape. Where would I go? What would I do? I knew that as a felon on the run, my carefree days of running the scenic roadways all over America would be over. What was left? Mexico? Europe? The South Seas? Where would I go and how would I get there? The only answer I could come up with was I'd have to depend on Jabez hiding me out for a while. I felt like I would soon enough figure out a long-term plan.

This new existence I'd been nourishing now for nearly three months was starting to feel a little shaky – no, a whole lot shaky. Still, God was in control and I would follow His lead.

I left the house for the gym at 5:30. By 6:00 most of my forty team members were on the court warming up, getting ready for another grueling practice, and what I noticed more than anything else, they were enjoying each other's company – they were becoming a real team. An amazing thing, I was thinking, right there in front of my eyes, forty of America's most hardened criminals, lifers (many of them), they were bonding as brothers, they were starting to believe in something bigger than themselves.

I grabbed Russell Burwell as soon as I saw him and by now, of course, I had no worries at all that any of the guards were on to us. We could talk freely about anything, just so long as we made sure no one could hear us. The routines and patterns I had been building with Russell, and with Bundy Trigget as well, were now paying off.

"Russell," I said, "Tonight's the night. We're getting out of here. We make our move after practice is over. You ready to go?"

"Yes sir, never been mo' ready in my life."

"Okay. Stay cool. We run a normal practice, nothing out of the ordinary. At the end when we break, you, me, and Trigget are heading for my office, just like normal, okay. But a minute later only you and me will be coming out. We are going to take Trigget out of the picture. We're not going to hurt him, just duct tape his mouth shut and tie him up. But first, we strip him and you put his uniform on. He's a big, strong man. Here's how we're going to handle him. I'm going to have him sitting at my desk looking at the playbook. When I wink at you, you are going to grab his sidearm out of his belt holster and you've got to say something really nasty, like, "Don't move or I'll put a bullet in the back of your head.'"

That's when it came to me – how I could extricate myself from the crime – the escape. Before, I was going to be an active participant in Trigget's take-down. Now, I saw a better way – I would be a victim too. I explained the new plan to Russell. "Say something similar to me, maybe, 'Coach, you keep your mouth shut. I can kill you quick.'" Then I explained the next step to him. "Order me to duct tape his mouth shut, strip his uniform, and then tape him to the chair, or you'll kill me dead. Got it? You've got the drop on both of us and you make me tape Trigget to the chair. If I don't, you'll kill both of us. You got nothing to lose."

"Yeah, I think I can do it, Coach."

"You sure?"

"Oh yeah, I can do it."

"Then, you order me out the door. That's important – that Trigget hears you order me out. From then on, you just follow me. Don't talk, don't look around, just follow me."

"Coach Finn, will I see my Lucille tonight?"

"I'm not sure. If not tonight, probably tomorrow morning. How does that sound?"

"Mighty good, Coach. Mighty good."

When practice buttoned up, the three of us walked across the gym to my little office. There normally would be about a ten to fifteen minute interim before guards started loading the team on a bus to escort them back to their cell blocks. That ten to fifteen minutes was all the time we had to make it happen. We had to move quickly. And we did. Burwell played his role perfectly. He had me and Trigget, both, convinced he'd put our lights out.

Trigget was taped to the chair like he was a mummy. Burwell and I came out of my office after only four minutes. None of the guards took special notice because, well, because to them it was Corporal Trigget. He (Burwell) did exactly what I had instructed him to do. He kept his head down a little, he didn't look around and he followed me out the back door of the gym to my car. We, me and Trigget, had been doing the exact same thing every night for almost two weeks now. It would take a few more minutes before some detail-oriented guard would ask himself, "Where is Burwell?" Hopefully it would take a few more minutes before he said to himself, "I better check the rest rooms, or the bus." Hopefully, my office would be the last place to check. That must have been what happened, because me and Burwell were out the main gate, and I was driving east towards Laurel Hill after only about nine minutes of total elapsed time.

215

I turned off the main road and picked up some back roads I had previously committed to memory. I was hauling you-know-what. I was getting Russell Burwell as far away from Angola as fast as I could. In twenty minutes, using the backroads, we had crossed into Mississippi and I picked up highway 61-north heading for Natchez. I drove five more minutes and spotted Jabez's truck sitting on the widened shoulder where a little shack was thirty feet away. That was the landmark we'd agreed on.

Russell jumped out of my car and climbed into the big truck. He had stripped Trigget's uniform and put on some things I had stuffed under the front seat for him. We didn't waste any time with niceties or chit chat. Jabez had the big truck rolling north, towards Tennessee. I figured that Russell Burwell's heart about jumped out of his chest when he got in the truck. I saw through the windshield there was a woman in there with Jabez, a black woman.

I didn't use the back roads on my way back to the prison. As soon as I entered Laurel Hill, I called the Warden's personal cell phone. "Warden, he's heading south. He just now let me go. I saw him get in a gray SUV. It looked like he carjacked it. I'm in Laurel Hill, I'm on my way back.

The warden said, "I'll be at the gate waiting for you."

It took me about fifteen minutes to drive back. The Warden was at the gate and his eyes were darker than I'd ever seen them. He and two guards approached my open window. "Get out, coach. We're going to have a little talk." There were sirens and horns howling. The prison was on lock down.

One of the guards got in my car and drove it away. The Warden and the other guard put me in the Warden's personal security SUV and the guard drove us to the building where the

Warden's office was. After we entered his office, the Warden dismissed the guard and claimed his throne behind his desk. There was no offer to use the comfortable chairs by the window tonight.

"You want to tell me why it was Burwell?" He wasn't overplaying it. Nothing dramatic or theatrical. It was almost as if we were out fishing somewhere, and he wanted to know why the fish weren't biting.

I said, "What do you mean?"

"Sit down," he said. "We're not in a hurry. We could sit here and talk all night." The blast from the horns outside threatened to erase his voice, and the sweeping arcs of the jumbo search lights invaded the office and waved through the darker corners of the room.

"Warden, I had no idea what he was up to. He grabbed Corporal Trigget's gun, and he threatened to kill both of us. He made me duct tape the Corporal to the chair after he'd put on Trigget's uniform. He said we're going to walk out of here to my car and if I made any kind of a move, he'd empty the gun in my back."

"And so, you just drove him right out of prison. Is that it?"

"What else could I do. He said he'd kill me."

He sat there, thinking. You could see the cogs and the gears grinding. It was then I noticed a vein up by his temple thumping to a lively rhythm. His eyes were someplace else, searching regions that were baffling him, rendering useless his thirty years of experience in law enforcement and corrections. It was then that I realized he had no evidence that I was part of the escape. Oh, he had plenty of suspicion, but no hard evidence.

He asked again, "Why Burwell? What was it about him? We've got six thousand other convicts you might have tried to spring. Why him?"

I continued to maintain the only defense I had – that I was completely snookered by Burwell and that he had totally surprised both me and Trigget and that he aimed the gun at us and made us do what he wanted done.

But the Warden was far from buying my story. He surprised me when he said, "You know what Trigget said – once we got him undone? I mean Burwell did a job on him. His entire head was double covered in duct tape, including his ears. The only thing open was a little hole for him to breathe through his nose. He said he heard you all talking, but he couldn't make any of it out."

"Sure we were talking. I was trying to tell Burwell to give it up - that he'd never make it out that gate."

"Really? That's what you were saying to him?"

"Sure I was. What else would I have been saying?"

I thought I had him. But then a guard hustled into the office. "Warden, you better take a look at this." He placed a laptop in front of the Warden, hit a few keys, stepped aside and said, "We just downloaded this from the central security computer. It's the hidden camera in the coach's office in the gym."

The Warden scooted up as close to his desk as he could get, and he punched in the highest audio level he could get and then he hit the play button.

I heard my own voice, "Don't forget. Don't look around, don't talk, just follow me out to my car."

The Warden picked up his desk phone and said, "Get me the State Police in Mississippi."

I said, "You got me. I'll give you everything you want." I was lying again, but I knew it was buying Jabez and Russell a little more time.

"I know where he is," I said. "He's holed -up five miles from Laurel Hill. Your guys or even the Sheriff can have him back here in one hour. Hear me out. I'll give you everything you want."

The Warden's phone chirped and I heard on the intercom, "Warden, I've got the Mississippi State Police for you."

Colfield said, "Cancel that. Tell them I'll get back to them."

"Yes sir."

"Where is he?" His eyes returned to that familiar pencil lead laser beam and I knew I wouldn't be able to stall much longer. I assumed he deployed his chase team and the dragnet on highway 61 leading south towards Baton Rouge because before he had any incriminating evidence on me, I had said that's the direction Burwell was headed – south. At that time he had no reason not to believe me. Now, he had plenty of reason to doubt anything I said.

Still, I was going to give it my best shot. "Ridgewell Road, five miles out of Laurel Hill. Turn right on Tucker Way, go two miles, cross a bridge. The old shack on the left. We were going to let things cool down for a week, and then I was going out there to get him and drive him into Alabama at night, and I'd be back in time for practice the next day."

The Warden got on his phone and had the chase team, the Louisiana State Police, and the K-nine unit all heading for Tucker Way. He picked up a pen and started jotting down some notes on a legal pad. We sat there about five minutes, me not saying a word. The Warden was on the phone with the chase team and I could tell that he was getting constant updates. After another five minutes, I heard him say, "Repeat what you just said, Captain. I want to put this on the speaker."

The next thing I heard was a voice that seemed to be hollow and metallic but was certain of what it was saying, "Warden, we followed Ridgewell Road all the way out. There is no Tucker Way turn off out there or any other turn off that crosses a bridge after two miles."

"Copy that Captain. Forget the dragnet to the south. Focus all your attention to 61 north and call the Mississippi State Police up there."

"Copy that, Warden."

Sonny Colfield stood up and had the yellow legal pad in his hand. He walked over to the two nice, comfortable chairs near the window and said, "Sit over here, Coach." I took a seat near him and he handed me the legal pad he'd been making notes on. A heading across the top of the page said: Potential Felony Charges Against Finnegan Weaver. Under the heading were four entries:

Conspiracy to cause a prison escape - 20 years to life
Assault and Battery on a correctional officer - 10-20 years
Aiding and abetting a fugitive from justice - 10-20 years
Conspiracy to embezzle the State of Louisianna in a
fraudulent business scheme – 10-20 years

Sonny said, "Let's see, Coach Finn, I believe you told me you are sixty-eight years old." As he was talking, the gray, spooky searchlight beam shadows floated around the room only to be speared by intense white light flickers and shimmers. Those were the ones I thought might go right through me.

"You know, if you live another twenty years, we're only going to get *that much* out of you. Think about it, Coach, only one fifth, twenty percent of the sentence you will draw. That's all we'll get out of you. Seems a shame, the great state of Louisiana will be deprived of eighty years of justice, pay-back, redress that we are entitled to. And, you know what? Once you are sentenced here to Angola, I'll make it my single priority in life, to see that every second you are here will be the closest thing to hell on earth that a man could conceive of. And, have no illusions, Angola will be your home. I can guarantee it."

Sonny got up and stood over by the window. "What a shame. That gym over there was to have been the place that real change here at Angola might have been started. The kind of money you lied about could have really got us moving to improve everything here. Everything: health care, vocational training, advanced education, recreation, legal services, everyday living conditions and more, much more could have been done. Damn it Weaver, I believed you. I put more trust in you than I have anybody on my staff. Your plan to hook us up with the NBA was beautiful. You sold me totally. I bought every word of it. I had some confidential, discreet conversations of my own with the owners of the New Orleans Pelicans. They confirmed what you slid by me. They said if the right man was running the show, it was all very doable and in fact *should* be done. They knew about you, Weaver. They said if anybody could pull it off, it was you."

I felt like the door was opening just a crack. Maybe there was still a little light at the end of the tunnel. I said, "I could still pull it off, Warden."

"Oh no you don't! Put a lid on it. I don't want to hear it."

"Warden, the reason I planned Burwell's escape is because he's an innocent man. You may never have seen his file. I don't know. There were two witnesses that said Burwell acted in self-defense, but they were the wrong color. They were black. The four witnesses whose testimony prevailed; they were white."

He stood there at the window; his skinny frame appeared to vibrate a little. I didn't know if he was peeing in his pants, or if a snake had crawled up his leg. He turned back to look at me. "My God! I remember now. We get so many of them. Stuff like this happens all the time. My wife told me she dreamed he was about to be shot, but he picked up an ax and caught the man on the side of his head. We get so many of them. Burl Cain was still the warden then. I was an assistant warden. I remember, it was the very day Russell Burwell came into the receiving unit. The warden drove over there himself. He made sure that Burwell got a work assignment in one of the shops, not in the fields or, God forbid, the cell blocks. Normally a new convict won't get a shop assignment for five years or much longer. It was the only time I'd ever seen the Warden Cain do something like that. Twenty- three years he was the warden. That was the only time."

"Move the search back to the south," I said. "Give Burwell a chance. He's with his wife. I mean right now, he's back with his wife. I saw her. God's watching us right now, Warden. He's watching you and me."

He walked over to his desk and picked up the phone. "Captain, I've got extremely credible information. Shift the entire search for the escapee back to the south. We're wasting time and resources in Mississippi."

FIVE YEARS LATER

Sometimes when a man gets off his duff and does the one thing he was meant to do, I suppose you might say, he changes his existence. Whether or not Sonny Colfield's existence changed the night Russell Burwell escaped from Angola Prison, I couldn't say. Sonny Colfield and Burl Cain, both of them, faced with an impossible responsibility in the first place, both of them looked the other way just for a flicker of a second. By doing so, they changed the existence of a betrayed and unremembered soul. Betrayed and unremembered by everyone, except, of course, Lucille.

As for me, my return to coaching lasted five years. That's when Warden Colfield and I rewarded Bundy Trigget with the head coaching job of the Angola Cowboys. Bundy had been my assistant coach all five years. He used to make me laugh when he'd jab me with, "Don't tape my mouth shut, Coach", after he'd said something stupid. Of course, he didn't often say anything stupid. He's a fine coach and getting better all the time.

The Angola Cowboys became the biggest basketball attraction since the Harlem Globetrotters. We were in demand for exhibition games all over the world. The NBA, of course, was where the big bucks were and by the time I left the team, we were scheduling no less than thirty games a year with the likes of the Boston Celtics, the Los Angeles Lakers, the New Orleans Pelicans, and many of the rest. We never played a game off the property of the Angola Prison. The Louisiana legislature never relented to the pressure to change the law and allow our convict team to play outside the razor wired fences. By the end of my second year, we had built a beautiful, modern 20,000 seat arena inside the wire. Most games were filled to capacity with basketball fans from everywhere you could possibly imagine. The money we raised revolutionized prison reform, not just at Angola, but in the entire penal system in Louisiana. Some say existence change isn't possible. I say, come to Angola and take a look.

These days my morning runs with Oscar have dwindled down to only one or two a week. He just doesn't have the snap in his legs to go out with me every day. I keep my eyes open you know, my radar turned on, my senses sharp for the day the good Lord may send me back out on the roads again, pushing the limits of my new existence and doing my best to complete any assignment He may give me.

Jabez checks in with me every now and then. He says he's still getting assignments on a regular basis. When he has a little extra time, he says he likes to spend it with a wonderful couple from Louisiana that have been living in a beautiful home he and the man had built on his eighty acres in the East Tennessee mountains.

And it was just the other day I got a call from Percy. A lot of that same old interstellar racket of banging and colliding galaxies was in the background. We talked for a pretty good while. I felt like I didn't want the conversation to end. I couldn't stop myself. I had to ask him the question. "Percy," I said. "Tell me please, are you *really* just a switchboard operator?" The whirling cacophony of stardust, planets, and galaxies disappearing into black holes was threatening to wipe Percy's signal out, just like it had done before. The last thing I was sure I heard him say was, "There's always more than flesh and bone." But then, there were nonaudible vibrations of His voice. I guess I felt it, maybe better than actually hearing it, "I go to prepare a place for you."

About the Author

Gary H. Baker grew up in Louisville, Kentucky and is proud to claim his status as an "original baby boomer". The class of '46 was just that, and it marched off into the 60s as a force to be reckoned with. While some protested, and some sought peace and love, Gary did a four-year enlistment in the Navy and pulled a tour of duty off the coast of Vietnam. He later earned an undergraduate degree from the University of Hawaii and a master's degree in alternative education from Indiana University. Along the way, Gary worked as a bouncer, bartender, teacher, coach, coffee salesman, insurance salesman, financial services broker, lawn care business owner, and truck driver. Gary currently calls himself a novelist.

In 1986, Gary ran two thousand seven hundred miles in four months to promote the Just Say No clubs, the forerunner to DARE (Drug Abuse Resistance Education). Gary sees his writing as an attempt to follow God. Jesus is his Savior, and Gary will tell you quickly that he (Gary) falls short most of the time, but that won't keep him from trying again.

Other books by Gary H. Baker

The Truck Driver Series:

Rookie Truck Driver

West Bound, Hammer Down, Trouble in Montana

Truck Dreams

IF My People

Short Stories:

The Big Ride

Times and Places

The Springdale Series:

Ron and the Rhythm Aces, The Black Jacket
Boogie

Fullness of the Times

For more information, go to garyhbaker.com

Made in the USA
Columbia, SC
03 November 2022